The First Team

F. A. Ludwig

PublishAmerica
Baltimore

© 2011 by F. A. Ludwig.
All rights reserved. No part of this book may be reproduced, stored in a retrieval system or transmitted in any form or by any means without the prior written permission of the publishers, except by a reviewer who may quote brief passages in a review to be printed in a newspaper, magazine or journal.

First printing

All characters in this book are fictitious, and any resemblance to real persons, living or dead, is coincidental.

PublishAmerica has allowed this work to remain exactly as the author intended, verbatim, without editorial input.

Softcover 9781462633173
PUBLISHED BY PUBLISHAMERICA, LLLP
www.publishamerica.com
Baltimore

Printed in the United States of America

Other titles by this author:

The Dragon Twins
The Voyages of Sara (Sequel)
The Halfling Princess
Lost Angel
Scout Kii-jin
Aisling's Woods

Chapter One

"Mom, would you please tell Charley to leave me be," Jamie pleaded, as he yelled down the stairs, making sure he was loud enough to be heard out as far as the front steps of the porch.

"Oh, grow up," Charley responded with, giving her brother a glare as she tossed her hair around towards her shoulder. "You know perfectly well you killed those poor fish all by yourself, you kept playing with that heater," pointing towards the corner aquarium with her chin. "I didn't do that."

"You did too, I saw you over there," Jamie responded, abruptly changing the returning glare to a forlorn expression as their mother finally arrived to end the squabble. "Mom, all my fish are dead."

"I didn't touch his silly fish, and he knows it," Charley said, crossing her arms and staring at her brother. "He's looking for excuses again, not that it does me any good to explain. Dad will take his side as always, the fair haired child."

"Did you touch his stuff?" Darlene asked, letting out a tired sigh while giving her rebellious daughter her usual inquiring look.

"Mom, the heater was making a noise and smelled funny, so I unplugged it. That's all."

"See, I told you, mom," Jamie let out, giving his mother another practiced look to go with his whine, "She was just trying to get away with something, like always."

"Now I have to go buy more fish, and a new heater. It's broke now."

"You stand anywhere the top of the stairs while I'm around, you'll know what its like to have something broken, you little lying weasel," Charley muttered, giving her brother a final look from icy blue eyes as she turned to leave.

"Hey, none of that, young lady." Darlene cautioned, shaking her finger at her. "We've gone through enough of those kinds of remarks lately. School let out on Friday, and here you are on Monday, bickering with your brother."

"I'm not putting up with this all summer. Just grow up. Do you understand me?"

"Fine, I'm out of here," Charley returned, not bothering to glance towards her brother's gleeful expression as she made her way down the hall. "I'll be outside."

"I'm going up to the park," she added, stopping to look back up the stairs at her mother as she grabbed her worn walking staff from its place behind the door. "Don't worry, I'll be back in time for dad to get out the belt, threaten me with violence and scar my tender spirit," letting the screen door slam behind her as she made her way down the front steps.

"Before we all sit down to a nice pleasant family dinner," she added quietly, wiping an eye as she found the sidewalk, and turned down its endless length.

Dodging the puddles left from yesterday's heavy rains, she quickly found the comfortable spot on her favorite park bench, leaning back to let the warmth of the sun fall on her face.

"Waiting for lightning to strike," a boy's voice said sometime later, bringing her upright with a start.

The First Team 7

"Oh, it's just you, Jacob," she let out with a gasp, recognizing the boy on the bike behind her, "You startled me. I didn't hear your squeaky brakes, I guess I was daydreaming."

"Yeah, I heard it all from old lady Miller when I went past. You're waiting for your dad to get home again. She heard it from her porch next door when you left," Jacob said, giving Charley a quick embarrassed glance as he brushed some wild hair from his face. "I know you prefer to be alone and all, but maybe sometimes someone to talk too might help."

"You're sixteen almost seventeen now, same as me. We're in the same grade in school," Charley replied, allowing a brief smile to show at his suggestion as she relaxed against the bench again. "Isn't that like talking to a mirror?"

"Oh, yeah, I sort of see your point," Jacob replied, reaching over to steady himself against the bench as he got off his bike. "I can at least walk you back though."

"It's about that time I guess," Charley said, slowly standing up and stretching. "I've sat here long enough, asking the Gods to strike me dead... without any success. Let's go around the long way, some things don't need be rushed."

"Ever feel like a misfit?" Charley asked, giving Jacob a quick look before letting her gaze drift back on the trees as they walked along, following the walkway along the edge of the woods.

"I can't exactly relate, you know," Jacob replied after a moment. "No sisters, or even a brother at my place. There's no competition at home. Most times, it's just me there. I'd be starved skinny if you didn't invite me over to supper from time to time."

"Maybe I just need to get away, do something different," Charley pondered aloud, looking up to see where they were before looking down at the weathered sidewalk they were following.

"To the end of the rainbow?" he asked, looking over to judge her expression.

"Or over it," Charley remarked softly, letting the silence between them return, listening to the rhythmic tapping of her walking stick on the sidewalk.

"You're the oddest girl I've ever met," Jacob finally came out with when nothing else was said. "When all the others in school were gushing over the preparations for the next dance, trying to grab all the new dresses of a certain color, you were found shopping for a new belt for your jeans. To the relief of many I might add," he said, showing a smile. "You're the prettiest, and they all know it, even if you don't act like it. If you miss the senior prom next school year, you'll have a perfect dance record. I wouldn't wait around for them to hand you a certificate of achievement over it.

"If some of us decide to go out for pizza, you're always grounded. You don't even carry a ten-pound purse around like everyone else or even have a cell phone, just that little belt pouch.

"You get some of the best grades on the tests, and won't even let anyone cheat off your paper."

"See, there's a list already. Told you I was a misfit," Charley sighed, showing her brief smile again, "You know I've never gotten along with kids in school very well. I guess I just don't do people. Besides, who needs a phone when there's no one in the world to call? There's no need to have something just because everyone else just has to have one. I'm not one of the sheep."

"What about emergencies?" Jacob asked. "What if something happened to you?"

"Would I be missed?" Charley mused, not expecting an answer, "I'd probably get a lecture, and the belt. Sometimes I figure I was born without that little gear in my brain marked *social*," not bothering to mention that getting smacked while wearing a dress can leave marks on bare legs.

"You're about to set a world record on getting grounded, and I'm beginning to think you don't really get along with anyone in school these days. You just tolerate them until they irk you into saying something rash," Jacob said, his attention wandering towards the old houses they were passing, "Your approach to others is like an evaluation of their spirit or something."

"It isn't always like that, sometimes they just don't believe a word I say. I've given up on trying to convince them otherwise."

"I'm getting used to the feeling I get when grounded, Jacob. The house falls quiet when they go out to eat, or to a movie. It's like I'm alone in the universe and I can get comfortable with who I am. I can travel to places in my mind," her thoughts interrupted as she followed his look down the street. "Who's that?"

"That's Mr. Jackson, he's one of those realtor guys. My mom talked to him a couple times last year, but dropped everything when the economy went haywire," Jacob replied, eyeing the older man.

"You were going to move away?" Charley asked, giving him a look before returning her attention to the man ahead of them.

"No, she just wanted to sell off one of her rentals. She finally decided to keep it and fix it up," Jacob said, watching as Mr. Jackson hung a small sign on one of the fence posts before getting back into his car.

"Help wanted," Charley read, glancing down at the small wooden sign as they drew abreast of it.

"You hiring, Mr. Jackson," Jacob asked, looking over to where the realtor was fussing with his briefcase.

"Oh, hey kids. No, the lawyer for the estate there," he muttered, giving them a quick glance before focusing back on his paperwork, "They wanted someone local. Nothing special, just that little sign you see there. Let me tell you, she's an odd one to work for."

"They need someone who can operate a bulldozer," Jacob said, looking out across the struggling lawn at the massive house. "That place has been empty for a long time."

"It's not that bad," Charley said, crossing her arms, looking at the imposing three story house as it sat silent amid the towering oaks, "It's old, no getting around that, but it looks sound, structurally speaking. I like it, and I just love that old gargoyle up there on the roof, it's got character."

"Some attention to the woodwork is needed maybe, and some paint here and there. That goes without saying," she added, still eyeing the house. "That place has been sitting there like forever. It looks like it's haunted."

"1901 to be precise," Mr. Jackson said, finally closing his case, and starting his car. "Built with solid eight inch oak and hickory beams, and lots of heavy planks. I'm told it has a full basement, a finished attic, and probably full of antiques. I'd show you, but I don't have a key."

"You going to try and sell it once it's fixed up?" Jacob asked.

"Wish I could, but it's not on the market. I could make a fortune just reselling the wood. They don't make them like that anymore."

"I guess not," Charley said quietly, glancing back down at the sign the car sped off.

"If it's that old, and empty... how come that place doesn't

have any broken windows, or trash anywhere?" Jacob asked, looking the place over before looking back at Charley who was still examining the sign, "And how come we've never noticed that thing you called it up there. I must have passed this place a million times, and I don't recall seeing that before. Its huge... and wicked mean looking. I think it's looking at you."

"Haven't got a clue, I don't wander this way all that often. Maybe there's a monster in there that got them when the beer bottles were brought out," Charley idly replied, "or maybe that gargoyle up there just decided to move in since it was empty, like with bats in the attic. Hey, *maybe* it's his house, and now he's checking out all the kids that walk past here."

"Yeah, whatever. What's the rest of it say," Jacob asked, peering over at the sign.

"The address, Barkley Building, Suite 401, that's downtown," Charley said. "Bring sign."

"What?" Jacob asked, giving her a look at what she had said.

"*Bring sign*, that's what it says on the bottom," Charley replied, giving him a look, "I don't make this stuff up. You don't believe me?"

"What is it with you red headed girls," Jacob said, leaning his bike against himself as he held up both hands in front as a defense. "I believe you, I didn't understand, that's all. Man, you're really on edge today."

"Yeah, well. I'm told I'm at that age... irresponsible, rebellious, combative," Charley said quietly, her attention still on the sign, "... and always on edge."

"Don't worry," glancing over at him. "I overheard my dad telling my mom that it'll pass, that I'll become this serious mature person one day. Personally, I thought I was getting worse."

"You sure?" Jacob asked getting his bike ready for them to continue. "For real?"

"You don't believe me?" Charley repeated, showing an expressionless face as she looked at Jacob. "I know what I heard. It surprised me too."

"Ah, look. Let's not get into a fight. The whole school knows you kicked Sandra's butt over something she said last week. It'd look bad if I lost, too," Jacob said haltingly, looking uncomfortable. "I don't want to get caught with you sitting on my back while my face gets pushed into the mud."

"Oh, you're safe, Jacob," Charley gave out with the wave of a hand, "You're the only one I know that's mentioned the way I look in jeans."

"You heard that?" Jacob asked, quickly blushing.

"Yeah, you and Jeffery shouldn't talk so loud in the back of the bus. You can hear it all from the front seat."

"I know you've got your mom waiting," giving her watch a glance. "Thanks for the talk. I'm feeling better about my fate," showing him another smile. "Next time you see Jeffery, you can tell him he has it all wrong. I don't like PJ's, or nightgowns, never did. I prefer to sleep naked."

Giving a wave as Jacob blushed a deeper red, she watched as he pedaled off without further comment, showing a brief wave as he turned the corner.

Turning back, she reached out and lifted the sign from the post by its slim chain, reading the message again as she held it, finally tucking it under one arm as she turned towards home, giving the gargoyle a final lingering glance.

Seeing the driveway still empty, she entered quietly, making her way up the stairs to her room without incident.

Carefully closing the door behind her, she flounced down

on the bed, still unmade from the morning. "Teddy, I hate this part... the waiting," she said, reaching out to poke the oversized stuffed bear next to her with a finger, "but, I've got you to keep watch over me," setting the sign in front of him with a sigh.

"Oh, before I forget," muttering as she knelt down beside the bed to reach between the mattress and the box springs, bringing out a zippered pouch.

"This is all that's left, Teddy," holding up the three $20's she had stashed away. "I was saving this for some new shorts and a top. Maybe it's a sign," smiling at her own wit as she glanced down at the sign once more, reaching out to run a finger over the words.

"*Bring sign*, now why would they say that?" she mused, sitting back down on the bed and leaning back against the pillows.

"*Charlotte*, I've called you down to supper twice. You sick or something?" Darlene asked from the open doorway.

"Oh. Sorry, mom. I must have dozed off," Charley replied, rubbing at her eyes as she hurriedly sat up on the edge of the bed.

"Your father is still waiting in the den, so go talk to him first," her mother added, moving aside to let Charley exit the room. "He's not pleased with you for what you did."

"Sure mom, he rarely is. Keep the door open, I'll probably be right back."

"Hey," Charley said, ending her pause outside the den by tapping on the door and letting herself in, "You wanted to see me, dad?"

"Yes," William sighed, lowering the newspaper to look over at her, "What's this I hear about some dead fish?"

"It was an accident dad, I swear," Charley said quietly, appraising his mood. "If Jamie says I killed all his fish, then it must be true. But it wasn't intentional, I was just checking the heater."

"I see," he responded, folding up the paper and setting it aside, unsure on how to handle this quick admission. "What do you propose we do to handle the situation?"

"No supper?" Charley said, giving him a wistful expression as she tucked her hands in back pockets of her jeans.

"That doesn't cover it, I'm still out of pocket over this," he said, leaning back in his chair. "Get serious with your proposition."

"Alright," digging down in her jeans pocket and bringing out her remaining funds as she walked over in front of him. "I figure this should cover it, and give him extra for some of those fancy tailed fish he's been harping about for the last month. Tell mom to take him to the pet store downtown for the new heater, not that department store she usually goes to, their brand of heaters are prone to overheating."

"I'm surprised," her father said, slowly taking the offered money. "You've changed."

"No, dad. I'm still me," Charley said stepping back, "I'm not interested in getting grounded for the summer, I'm considering getting a job."

"Oh, you've found a new family with kids to watch?" he asked, placing the folded money in his shirt pocket as he stood up.

"No, something different this time. I'm thinking its yard maintenance… that sort of thing… outside work. I want to go down and apply for it tomorrow."

"You talk to you mother about this yet," he asked, nodding them towards the door.

"No, it's new. I just found out about the opening this afternoon. I was planning on telling everyone if I got hired, and had the details."

"I see. Well good luck with your interview, something to keep you busy is a good thing," leading them into the dining room.

"I didn't hear you use the belt, dad," Jamie chimed out, giving his sister a sour look as they entered. "She killed all my fish you know. Every last one of them."

"It's been dealt with, so enough on the fish," his mother said, giving him a frown. "It's best for all concerned if you treated your sister with a little more respect."

"She's not my real sister, mom. She was adopted," Jamie let out, trying to cover his outburst with an innocent expression as he saw the reaction on everyone's face.

"I'm real enough to stomp your face into the mud out back," Charley came out with, using her low, quiet tone of voice. "Care to take a little walk before we have our dinner?"

"Enough, *Please?*" Darlene said, looking over to her husband. "Maybe you can take Jamie out looking for his heater, I've had about all I can take of these two for one day."

"I'll take care of it," William replied, keeping his eyes on Jamie, "We need to have some words exchanged."

"Don't worry yourself, mom," Charley said, looking up from where she had been staring at her empty plate. "I'm not feeling all that well, so I'll try to eat something later."

"Charlotte, he didn't mean anything by it, he's just in one of his moods," Darlene said, seeing that Charley was ready to leave the room.

"Sure, mom. No problem," Charley replied, giving Jamie her expressionless look, "Just one of his moods. I'm going to go lay back down for a while. Remember what I said about the store dad," turning to her father for a moment. "Don't get him another cheap one, they're just junk."

"I don't what to do for her," Darlene finally said, as Charley made her way up the stairs to her room.

"Well, she has something in mind. I'm sure she'll mention it when she's ready," William sighed, looking around at the evening meal. "Load me up," holding out his plate.

"What kind of heater do you need?" William asked, picking up his jacket and car keys.

"It's one of those green plastic kind, dad," Jamie said, beaming at the prospect of buying something with his father. "Mom bought it for me with the whole setup."

"Well, go get the old one, I'll see what the wattage rating is on it when we get there," William said, heading for the front door. "Be quick about it, I want to have to time to sit down and relax this evening when we get back."

"How was your fishing trip, bring one back?" Darlene asked, as the front door was swung open and Jamie flew in ahead of his father.

"Wait until you see, mom. I got the special long tailed ones, the kind I've been wanting," Jamie gushed, setting his bag down on the kitchen counter. "Dad spent a whole lot of money on them, and I got to pick out the ones I wanted."

"Did you remember to get a new heater, that was your main concern this afternoon, as I recall," she said, looking up at William as he came inside.

"Sure mom, dad has it. He didn't want me to drop it or anything. It's a professional kind, and once it's set up, I don't ever have to touch it."

"That's nice, dear," nodding as Jamie began to bring out

several clear plastic bags of water and fish from the bag. "Why don't you take them all upstairs and set them in the tank to get them adjusted. I cleaned it up for you while you were gone. Dad will be right up to get the heater set up for you."

"Boy, I'm having all my friends over tomorrow, they've got to see these," Jamie said, carefully picking up the fish and heading up to his room.

"What is it?" Darlene asked, noting the look on her husband's face. "I've seen that expression before."

"It can wait, I'll tell you later," William replied, the thoughtful look still on his face. "Did Charley tell you what she did to the old heater," stopping for a moment to hear her reply.

"Yes, she said it was making a noise and smelled odd, or strange," she replied, "Jamie keep saying she broke it, and killed all his fish. I guess when she unplugged it."

"Did she give you a different story," trying to determine the cause of his question.

"No, no, she told me she checked it. I was just thinking on something, that's all," William said, setting the old heater down on the counter. "Let me get the new one installed before he wets himself up there," he sighed, placing his jacket over the back of his chair. "I'll check on her before I come back down."

"Hey, dad. I gather from all the ooh's and ahh's I heard earlier that the aquarium is back in proper working order, its population restored," Charley said, looking up over her book as the door was tapped upon and slowly opened.

"I just wanted to let you know I talked to the clerk at the pet store."

"Yes?" brushing some of her hair away from her face to see him better.

"He told me it'd take several days for our size tank to heat up enough to kill any of those fish," William said, leaning against the doorframe. "I showed him the old heater, so I'd get the proper type to replace it with."

"Yeah," keeping her eyes on him. "That's best, dad. Those guys are pretty savvy when it come to the stuff they sell there."

"When he saw the melted plastic, he let out a low whistle of surprise," William said quietly, "I hadn't noticed it."

"It seems someone pulled the plug just in time to keep it from catching on fire. We could have lost the house."

"That would have been bad. I guess there must be somebody watching over us," Charley said, matching her father's quiet tone as she met his eyes, "Some kind of guardian or something."

"She says she'll snag a baked potato, later." William said, sitting down on the sofa beside Darlene with a sigh.

"I was surprised you didn't use the belt earlier," Darlene said, getting comfortable. "She hasn't done anything like that since she was twelve, that time she took one of your wrenches from the garage that night, and attacked that gas valve out back."

"Yeah, I remember," William said, looking thoughtful again at the memory. "She mangled that valve so bad it had to be replaced with a new one. I couldn't get it opened back up. We nearly froze that night as I recall. It was a bad winter."

"And she started those awful fits over wearing dresses ever since," Darlene said also thinking back. "I don't think she has a single one up there today. She won't let me take her shopping if I mention we're looking at dresses."

"Well, she has her own ways about her, that's for certain," William finally said, letting go of a troublesome thought,

patting Darlene on one leg as he turned his attention to the TV.
"Give her time."

"Wow, Teddy," Charley let out. "Look what the night fairy left us," picking up the still folded bills from the night table. "This is strange, we never got a rebate before," she mused, looking at the money.

"Good morning," Darlene said as Charley came down the stairs. "You've brushed your hair, and put it in a ponytail. Going somewhere?"

"Yeah, downtown," Charley replied, flinging the heavy mane around to her back. "I'm following a lead on a job for the summer, and I thought it might be best to show my face a little. You know, in case they want to know who they're hiring."

"All summer?" Darlene asked, trying to hide the relief she felt at the prospect.

"That's the impression I got, I'll know more when I get back," tucking the sign into a shoulder pouch. "I might have to stop and check out some work clothes if I get it, not sure yet."

"Is it office work, something you can do after school too?" her mother asked following Charley into the kitchen.

"Sorry to disappoint, but I think it's outside in the fresh air work, mom," Charley said, grabbing a banana off the counter. "You should toss that old heater before Jamie thinks he has two of them," sliding the melted heater left lying on the table towards her mother. "I think dad said it's a shock hazard or something last night."

"Oh yes, father knows best," her mother said, picking it up by the cord and letting the heater dangle. "It's history," as she dropped it into the trash can.

"Great," Charley said, walking out to the hall mirror to

give herself a final check before leaving. "I have my key, so I'll be back when I'm back."

"You'll be back in time for supper?" Darlene asked, standing at the door as Charley went down the front steps.

"Probably, mom but you know how the bus system is some days," she replied, turning onto her usual route down the sidewalk. "I'll try."

"Hey, Jacob," Charley said, surprised at seeing him waiting at the bus stop. "What's up, going to town, too?"

"Yeah," he said, looking a little uncomfortable at the sight of her. "I thought it'd be a good idea, you know… to see if you get that job."

"I see," replying as she turned to see the bus arriving. "I never mentioned it."

"Ah, well," Jacob gave out, following her onto the bus and dropping his change in the box. "I sort of went back to see that sign again, and it wasn't there, so I figured you took it."

"Yeah, what's the rest of it?" she asked, keeping her eyes on him. "What's the truth?"

"What makes you ask that," Jacob asked, beginning to look a little defensive as they found a seat together.

"Maybe because you've told everyone about a thousand times how your mom won't let you get any kind of after school job until your grades are better. So it's easy to suspect something else is going on here," Charley replied. "You barely missed having to attend summer classes again.

"So?" giving him an expectant look.

"So, I sort of ran into Jeffery and Walsh about a block from home," Jacob said, not looking over to meet her gaze. "They told me the sign wasn't there."

"That's what I thought. So they heard about a job from you,

and rushed over to claim it," she said quietly, leaning back against the seat.

"What were they going to do, fight over it to see who got to keep it?" she finally asked, glancing over in Jacob's direction.

"I guess," Jacob replied, staring at the back of the seat in front of him. "When they couldn't find it, Walsh decided to try for it anyway. He was going to say he lost it."

"Or try to take it away from me… that's why you're here this morning," Charley said in a low voice, glancing back at the other passengers.

"He isn't here."

"He had his mother give him a ride," Jacob said, sounding a little glum. "He wanted to get there first."

"This place is nice," Charley exclaimed, feeling the cool air rushing over her as they entered the lobby of the building. "I've never been in here before."

"Me neither," Jacob said, looking around for Walsh, "I think this is where you come to get a divorce."

"Don't you mean the Court House?" Charley replied, admiring the decor while leading them over towards the elevators. "It's got that early European, sort of Pagan-gothic touch to it."

"Nice teeth," Jacob sighed, looking at a statue of a rearing dragon as they passed it. "Some of this stuff looks old, like it came from a museum."

"Oh, wow. Hold up," Charley suddenly said, pulling at Jacob's sleeve. "Check this out."

"Impressive," Jacob finally said, staring up at the huge statue that dominated one corner of the lobby. "Don't tell me, let me guess… it's a Gargoyle."

"Isn't he's magnificent," Charley sighed, admiring the

detail of the artistry as she walked over to it, "Man, will you take a look at those fangs, and the size of those wings. He must be at least nine feet tall and covered with muscles. I just love him."

"Come on, you can drool over him afterwards," Jacob said, hooking her arm and pulling her back while looking back at the ancient statue. "You shouldn't have touched it, the eyes are following you now. There's probably another kind waiting for you upstairs."

"Another one of those?" Charley asked, reluctantly letting herself get led back to the elevator while still looking back at the statue.

"I meant the lawyer," Jacob said, punching the button for the fourth floor for her.

"His eyes were made of stone, you know," Charley said. "Just like the rest of him."

"Hey, speaking of eyes, did you see look that guy just gave you?" Jacob asked, trying to look around the corner at the departing darkly dressed figure as the doors began to close. "If looks could kill, you'd be toast."

"Look who's here, another smiling face," he whispered as the doors opened with a chime to reveal an office that spread out before them.

"I figured as much," Charley replied quietly, looking around them at the furnishings. "This place is really wild looking, too."

"Man, what do you know, the competition actually showed up," Walsh let out, not bothering to move over on the sofa he had lounged himself on. "I don't know why you wasted your bus money. I heard you were grounded, again."

"No, not this time." Charley replied as she finally brought

her gaze around to him. "I guess the Gods have other plans for me. I still live and breathe."

"You know, my dad's a Doctor, I can get some lotion to smear over your bruises. All you have to do is… ah, *expose* them to me," Walsh said with a leer, giving her form a lingering glance.

"Did I miss a button or something?" Charley asked, before checking down at her top, seeing where his eyes went first.

"Thanks for checking, I wanted to make a good impression," she added, displaying her expressionless face to him. "I'm even wearing my best bra."

"Ah," Jacob interrupted with. "So, where's the receptionist?" taking a hand from a pocket and waving it towards the empty desk that dominated the side of the room that faced the elevator.

"She's out, read the card on the desk, dummy," Walsh said, not bothering to look at Jacob. "Yeah, I like to help," running his gaze down Charley's curves again, "Maybe I can adjust something for you."

"Sure," Charley said, moving one foot back as she turned slightly towards him. "Why don't you step over here, and try that. I think I know what gets adjusted first. My dad explained it to me."

"May I help you?" a voice suddenly asked, the French accent seeming to leave an echo around the room.

"Yeah," Walsh blurted out, trying to recover from his surprise at her sudden appearance as he quickly stood up. "I was here first, I'm here for the job."

"The job?" the young dark haired women asked, placing a folder down and settling herself behind her desk while giving Walsh her attention.

"Yeah, you know. The one on the sign," he said, walking over closer to her.

"Oh yes, that one. I recall it now," the girl replied, sitting back as if appraising Walsh. "Did you bring the sign?"

"No, somebody stole it from me, while my back was turned," Walsh said, his eyes shifting over towards Charley for a brief moment before focusing back on the girl. "So, I don't have it anymore."

"I'm sorry to hear of your unfortunate loss... Mr....?" she responded with, never taking her brown eyes off of him.

"Oh, Walsh, Walsh Edwards. My father's a doctor down at City Hospital. Maybe you've heard of him."

"No... I'm sorry Mr. Edwards, I haven't. Our clients rarely need to see a doctor, or a hospital once we've visited them.

"Tell me, Mr. Edwards, what size dress do you normally wear?" she asked, bringing out a notepad and picking up a pen from the desk as she leaned forward. "I'll need your breast size as well."

"Dress?" Walsh asked, his confusion showing on his face.

"Of course," she replied, her eyes traveling over him as she leaned back and brought the pen up to her lips, "and we'll have to see how you look after the legs are shaved, so you'll have to drop those pants for me."

"Hey, wait a minute," Walsh let out, taking a step back away from the desk as he held up a hand. "I just wanted the job, nothing else."

"Yes, I understand," the girl said, nodding at his expression. "You were here first, so I'm giving you every consideration possible. You are aware that the opening is for a fashion model, *Oui?*"

"We'll have to do something about your lack of cleavage..." examining him again, "but you said your father is a doctor, so I think we can come up with something that will work... less out of pocket expense for you that way. I understand the implants they use today are identical to natural breasts."

"A model?" Walsh repeated, taking another step backwards. "I thought this was for some stupid yard work… painting, and crap like that."

"I'm sorry, Mr. Edwards. No crap. I had assumed you had read the other side of the sign when you had possession of it. It clearly states the job requirements and prerequisites, the first being that you must look acceptable wearing a formal evening dress."

"There was no mention concerning any yard work," she added, giving him a light smile of compassion. "As I said, we're willing to work with you if you still wish the position. We use our models in the European market where they're much more accepting, so there's a good chance your friends won't see you in a magazine locally."

"No, thanks," Walsh uttered, looking the room before bringing his attention back to the girl. "You can keep the job, I ain't getting myself turned into some kind of weirdo, wearing some dress for somebody. Forget that crap," he came out with, giving Charley and Jacob a look of disgust as he headed for the open elevator doors. "I'm gone."

"That didn't take very long," the women said quietly, almost to herself as the doors silently closed behind Walsh and she turned her attention to Jacob.

"I suppose you're next."

"No, not me," Jacob responded with, holding up both hands and stepping back towards the elevator. "I'm just here to keep my friend company, that's all."

"Yes, I see," she said, finally bringing her attention to Charley. "Come here please, over in front of the desk will do."

"There wasn't anything written on the other side of that sign," Charley said nervously as she moved closer as directed.

"I've read it," bringing out the sign from her pouch. "He never saw it."

"You're the one," the woman said quietly, leaning forward to take the sign and place it down on the desk in front of her.

"What is your name, my dear?" she asked leaning back again.

"It's Charley, my last name is MacIntire." Charley said, beginning to feel some discomfort under the woman's appraising eyes.

"Remove your clothing, Charlie," she suddenly said, pointing towards Charley's top with her pen. "I need to see."

"Yes... you're in a room with a stranger, your male friend is over there waiting with baited breath, suddenly hopeful to see something he's been dreaming about, and there is a job position at stake... all this I understand. What is your choice," she asked, tapping the sign with her pen.

"I don't really like dresses." Charley said quietly, considering her options.

"That's acceptable, you're not expected to purchase one. Please, I'm waiting. I'd like to see if you have the cleavage we're looking for."

"With a name like Charlie, I'm paid to see if you meet our needs, I'm sure you understand," she added.

"Oh, sure. I guess I do," Charley replied, glancing back over to where Jacob was standing. "Ah, right here?"

"Yes, and I can assure you, there are no camera's in here. It's just us."

"I didn't realize this would be a modeling job, I've never done that kind of work before," Charley said, reaching up and pulling the band from her hair so it spread across her shoulders as it fell it's full waist length, before reaching down the hem of her top, holding her breath as she quickly lifted it up free of her head and arms.

"Relax, let your arms hang down freely at your sides," nodding and smiling at Charley's expression, "Excellent form," standing up and coming around to the front of the desk, giving Charley her attention. "Great bone structure, and skin tone. You have good height as well."

"We won't have to worry about any tan lines for the swim suits, I see... How bold are you?" she suddenly asked, leaning back against the desk, her eyes on Charley.

"I can be as bold as I need to be," Charley replied, fidgeting with a length of hair. "I've been studying Tahitian dancing for the last six years. I've actually displayed more wearing less while dancing. What kind of modeling was this again?"

"It's not what you, or your friend over there might be thinking," the girl responded with, showing a brief smile at the question.

"Why do you want a job?" she asked, her tone of voice changing to a more serious level.

"I want to get away from home," Charley said, trying to be as honest as she could, keeping her eyes on her.

"Perhaps you feel you don't fit in, that there's something else more important, and you're wasting your time dealing with children?" she asked in low voice, nodding at the reaction on Charley's face. "Maybe we can give your dreams some reality. Give me your bra, I still need to see if you're a Charlotte or a *Charlie*."

"I thought you said the implants look just as natural," Charley said, hesitating as she slowly moved her hands behind her to unfasten the catches, making sure her back was to Jacob.

"So they do," the girl suddenly said, stopping Charley with an upraised hand, looking past her at Jacob who had backed himself up against the elevator doors. "You can stop by Charlotte's house and let her mother know she'll be late?"

she asked, nodding at him as the doors opened to accept him.

"Tell her she got a new job, one that she can do after school hours as well."

"That should please her to no end," she added quietly, turning to give Charley a brief smile.

"This isn't for a modeling job, is it?" Charley asked, refastening the catches when she saw the girl's expression change as the elevator swallowed Jacob, and the doors closed behind him.

Chapter Two

"No, Charlotte, it isn't. You can call me Anastasia, or Anna for short," Anna said, walking over to Charley and placing a hand on her shoulder, "Now everyone who thinks they know something about your new job, doesn't know anything. You're now in the international modeling business as far as they are concerned."

"I had to come up with something quickly when I saw that first boy come into the elevator. He didn't look the type who would get into a dress."

"A thousand questions, I know," Anna said, raising a hand as Charley opened her mouth. "First, we have some papers, just in case someone wants to check," walking around to the desk and opening a folder lying on top. "They're all filled out, I just need your signature at the bottom of these, and I need to know your ring size."

"Ah," Charley said, slowly accepting the pen in to her hand, "I'm still a minor, and I don't even know what the job is, or how much it pays… the hours… nothing."

"Oh, and I think I wear a size five."

"We'll get your father to sign it tonight," Anna said, trying to slow down and explain. "He owes you. You will set the hours for the most part once your training period is over, and

I'll have to explain that as we go. The pay is five thousand."

"That's not even enough for me to get my own car, and pay for a dinner out, too," Charley said, looking up as she was about to sign where Anna had indicated. "I was really hoping for a bit more. I just got my license and I'm getting tired of having to take the bus."

"Five thousand a *week*, plus bonuses," Anna said, nodding towards the paper.

"What do I have to do, kill somebody?" Charley asked standing up in surprise, her eyes widening at the amount.

"Something like that," Anna replied, "Your bank account has already been set up, so you need to sign that smaller card there as well, and I'll still need your bra."

"What for?" Charley asked, lifting up the signed papers and handing them over to Anna.

"Your scent. I know, it raises even more questions, but you'll understand what I'm saying later," Anna said. "He already knows what you look like, but they use the scent to track when it's dark… the pheromones you understand. They say *Charlotte*, and not just 'human girl'."

"Doesn't a lawyer have to see those," Charley asked as Anna brought out a seal from the desk drawer.

"I'm the lawyer," Anna said affixing the seal imprint to the paper Charley had signed first. "Now, we get your father to sign below yours, and you're all set as far as any paper trail."

"What do those others say?" Charley asked, noting the extra papers Anna placed on top of the one she had marked.

"Lawyer talk for using your smiling face and alluring form, within the stated laws of the countries in which you will be working, passport, excreta, excreta," Anna said, placing a paper clip on them before setting them into a folder.

"You mean in case I ever get asked to pose naked on a

bearskin," Charley asked, thinking on her mother's reaction.

"I didn't think of doing that, thanks for the idea," Anna said, looking down into another drawer and bringing out a folded bundle. "We'll come up with some shots, build your portfolio just as if you were working in the business. It makes a good cover, no pun intended. Let's plan on doing that this afternoon. I'll have a photographer and consultant on hand."

"I took the liberty of listing a different pay scale on those papers than what I told you, so it seems to fit your new job position."

"Here's a tee shirt, I think you'll like it," Anna said, handing over the folded item she had been holding. "I'll trade you for that bra. I have other clothes waiting upstairs for you as well."

"Hey, there's a gargoyle on here," Charley said, examining the embroidered design on the shirt as she unfolded it. "I've always liked them for some reason. I actually saw one on a roof the other day. There's a really great looking one downstairs."

"Yes, so I was told," Anna said, glancing over at the shirt. "They tend to move those things around down there, but you're not technically correct. If they're not attached to a building, they're called a *grotesque*. I had to look it up."

"All of your new clothes will have that on them somewhere, and the term 'gargoyle' works just fine in the modern sense. Consider it as a family crest, a badge you wear," holding out a hand for the bra.

"You have an accent, were you born in France," Charley asked, delaying the moment.

"No, I was raised there from childhood, I was born in Russia," Anna replied. "I'm one of those imports."

"That was part of a test, wasn't it?" Charley asked, thinking on the new word before pulling the new shirt on over her head and tugging it down. "Back when Jacob was here."

"Yes, you didn't even blush. I expected as much," Anna said, tucking the bra into a manila envelope along with the signed bankcard. "I know how the dancers dress in Tahiti."

"I know I'm rushing things a bit, but he makes me a little nervous when he gets impatient. He's been waiting for some time."

"Excuse me for a moment," Anna said, walking with it in hand over to closed doorway set into the back of the room.

At her tap, it opened and she lifted the envelope, a hand taking it from her and after a minute or so, handing back a small item in return before re-closing the door.

"Sorry, I'll explain more as we go, but he had asked for that," looking down at her desk, deciding on what to do next.

"He?" Charley asked, glancing back at the closed door. "The boss?"

"Oh, no," Anna quickly said, "It's someone you'll be working with, more like a senior partner. As I mentioned, it's only the scent on it that's of interest here. It's going to be returned."

"Oh, here before I lose it. This is yours to wear as long as you're with the firm. It's not to be removed," holding out her hand to reveal a heavy looking, dark silver ring on her palm. "Ever."

"It didn't have to be the bra," Anna said as Charley examined the ring, "It was that or something else, so I chose for you."

"Oh, that's fine," Charley said in a rush, looking over at the comment. "What a way to start a new job."

"Sure is," Anna said, nodding her head in agreement and showing a smile, "Weird, I know. I'm going to ask for a raise after this one, but you should have been here for the Eagle. That one I thought was cute."

"This is some fine craftsmanship," Charley said, peering closely at the figure on the ring before sliding it on her finger. "There's a gargoyle on it too. Perfect fit."

"You said someone already knew what I looked like, he's seen a picture?" Charley asked, pleased with the feel of the weight of the ring on her hand.

"No…" Anna said, almost absent mindedly as she gathered a few items from the desk. "On occasion, you leave your bedroom blinds open just a bit. He mentioned he saw you in your, ah… night attire," giving Charley a pointed look, before adding a smile. "I guess he liked your fashion sense."

"My room is up on the second floor. Do you have a photo or something of him, maybe I've seen him hanging out around the roofs in the neighborhood," Charley asked, raising an eyebrow.

"You'll recognize him when you see him," Anna said, giving the shirt another quick glance before taking Charley's hand again. "I'm glad you're finally here. You're hired. Come on, it's time to get to work. You're on the clock."

"You said upstairs before, I thought this was the top floor," Charley said, glancing at the control panel as they both entered the elevator.

"That's for the tourists to use," as the doors closed and the car rose up with a soft whirl. "Your ring will grant you access to anything and everything," Anna explained, "You don't have to go waving it around in the air, just step in and it'll bring you here. Everyone you meet in the company will take note of it, so you won't have to explain anything."

"Wow," Charley finally managed to say, looking around at the dark paneled room before them.

"Welcome to the office, it's empty right now," Anna said, leading her over to a wide fur draped sofa. "You might encounter a few folks passing through when you come to visit, other ring bearers such as yourself. You'll note the different designs they carry over time, the others are what you might call office staff, the busy little bees that do the work behind the scenes."

"Like him?" Charley managed to get out, the sight of the small dwarf-like person holding her attention as he suddenly appeared beside them, handing a small envelope to Anna, before giving Charley a slight bow of respect as he quietly turned and departed.

"Here, your bank card," Anna said, holding up a small envelope. "Yes, that's Granddon. He's worked for the company since the beginning. If you have questions, he's the one to talk to. His office is around to the north side of the building."

"You will discover that your account is active, and an advance of six months has been accredited to it," Anna explained, nodding towards the plastic card Charley found in the envelope. "You might not want to mention that part to friends or family. Just tell them you got a signing bonus."

"Six months pay? Are you kidding me?" Charley replied, trying to figure the sum in her head. "All I've done is show up. That's over a hundred thousand dollars!"

"One twenty," Anna said, glancing down at her watch, "You get paid every six months, and will be given a year's salary should you ever decide to retire. The company covers most needs when you're on the job…rooms, meals, and any incidentals. Keep your receipts."

"It's nearly noon, how about we do lunch somewhere, and then let it settle before getting those photos done."

"Before we leave, let's lose the jeans too," Anna mused, giving Charley's appearance another glance. "I have a few items for you to try on."

"I can't believe how I look," Charley finally said, still admiring herself in the tall mirror, running a hand down the high-waisted pants, "They're so soft, and these boots are the most comfortable shoes I've ever worn," peering down at her new footwear.

"I like the effect," Anna said, nodding at the sight. "Those pants show off your form better, and with that flat dancer's stomach of yours, the top lets everyone know you're pure Charlotte."

"There's something that goes with it, helps keep the men from tripping over something as they wander past you," Anna added, setting the hair brush she had been holding on the small wooden table beside them. "Perfect."

"This is yours as well," Anna said, grabbing a jacket from a rack as they passed it going out the dressing room. "Dove grey, your favorite color."

"Nice," Charley said, her eyes widening at the sight of the black Mercedes that pulled up to the front entrance, the employee handing over a set of keys to Anna as he passed her. "You travel in style."

"Oh, this one isn't mine, it's yours. I thought I'd surprise you a little bit more, especially since you're new to the job," Anna said, gesturing her towards the passenger door. "You'll need to have your license in hand before you get the keys, those insurance folks are awfully picky these days."

"This is mine?" Charley exclaimed in a low voice as she slid into the seat and glanced around at the interior. "I had no idea. It smells brand new."

"You should learn to read the fine print," Anna said, sharing the moment with her before starting the engine.

"You can always tell when they're new, there's no gas in the tank," she added, leaning forward to peer at the gauge. "I guess we'll take care of that first."

"Why all this stuff?" Charley asked, trying to feel comfortable while they waited for their food order to arrive by running a finger over the gargoyle emblem on the jacket draped over the chair beside her.

"It comes with the job," Anna said, "I have my own car as well."

"Yeah, but I mean, it's like you guys have been waiting for me to show up or something. Those papers already had my name on them," Charley said, looking over at Anna. "You knew who I was before I even stepped into the building, and that sign was set out just as I was getting close."

"He wanted you to begin last year, but we told him it was too soon. We thought next year would be better... so here we are, in the middle," Anna said, sitting back in her chair. "We didn't spy, you were... *monitored*."

"Isn't that the same thing?" Charley asked, trying to understand. "You said someone even looked through my window."

"No, legally speaking," Anna replied, showing a smile, "and the peek through the blinds wasn't requested or required, that naughty boy did that himself."

"We've known where you were since you were adopted."

"Ah, here we go," Anna said, leaning back as their meals were set in front of them with a flourish, not meeting Charley's eyes.

"You're not going to tell me some things, are you?" Charley asked, keeping her attention on Anna.

"Some things, I simply don't know," Anna replied, looking over to her. "The rest will come out as we go along."

"Well then, if modeling isn't the job... What is?" Charley asked, picking up her fork. "Can you tell me that?"

"Doing what you've been doing all along is a big part of

it, helping others in a manner of speaking," Anna said, before taking a taste of her salad. "You've always known when trouble was about to happen, you have natural gifts."

"Your adopted parents never understood that, they saw you as the willful one, the wild child. I must admit, taking that wrench to the gas valve was clever, but the cost was high."

"There was always a price to be paid," Charley said, thinking back. "At least the house didn't explode that night."

"How do you feel about dealing with problems caused by others, I don't mean the natural ones you've been dealing with. The people who go out of their way to harm the innocent," Anna asked, lowering her fork to await the answer.

"You mean protecting them, like children and such?" Charley asked, before attacking her own plate.

"We tend to see the innocent as being the children, but I meant everyone who is victimized by the evil that lurks in the hearts of so many."

"Wait a minute…" Charley said, setting her fork down and sitting back in her chair. "You don't mean protecting the innocent, more like eliminating the threat to them, like I did with the heater by pulling the plug. Am I right on this?"

"Essentially. It could be seen as a matter of semantics, but once you find the, ah… heater, we have someone else in mind who will actually pull the plug, if I can use that analogy," Anna said, giving Charley a close look. "You'd work together, as a team."

"Oh, wow," Charley said in a low voice, thinking on what was being said. "The senior partner. No wonder I got a new car. This is like super agent stuff."

"Does my car come with an ejection seat?" she asked, her eyes widening at the thought.

"Not that kind of super agent," Anna said quietly. "You got

the deluxe edition, with tinted windows, GPS tracker, stereo… stuff like that. It's intended for your personal use."

"I see," Charley said, still thinking on what Anna had said. "So… how do I, I mean *we* get around to find the bad guys?"

"I should wait on that until tomorrow, that's when your training will begin," Anna said, nodding towards Charley's plate. "Eat up, you're paying for us this time. It's a long standing tradition."

"Wait a minute, hold up," Charley said, her eyes widening again at a sudden thought. "The bad guys have natural gifts too, don't they?"

"Some of them," Anna said. "Sometimes they know what's coming their way, too. Those types are few, but that makes the assignment more difficult. They can be as slippery as eels."

"And dangerous, I bet." Charley said, picking up her fork again.

"Yeah, that too," Anna said, tapping her fork against her plate. "I think I need some wine."

"When did this tradition begin," Charley asked, proudly presenting her new card as they prepared to leave.

"Ever since the time I forgot to bring any money with me," Anna said, showing a smile. "Now, I just come up with a tale, and they gladly pay."

"You're awful." Charley said, returning a grin.

"Yes, but it usually takes them a few encounters to realize that." Anna said, picking up Charley's jacket for her.

"The studio I'm using for you is an hour away," Anna said, unlocking the car doors. "They already know your size, so there should be a good selection of clothing and props."

"You said something about the European market, will some of these actually show up in a magazine?" Charley asked, getting comfortable in her seat.

"Yes, a few will run them, so you can have them lying about in your room." Anna said, glancing over.

"Over here, I'm not supposed to have cleavage showing at my age, whose standards are they using for my photo shoot?"

"In Europe, they understand we are all born naked, and for the most part, have no issues on being seen that way," Anna said, giving Charley a smile. "A few will no doubt capture some of your natural beauty, as intended. These are modeling professionals, not voyeurs with a camera. I think you'll be impressed with their work."

"I already have several of you taken while dancing in full costume… with some very fine cleavage."

"My mom's going to want to see me, if I'm in a magazine." Charley said later, turning towards Anna as she rested against the seat back.

"It's about time she felt some pride in you," Anna said, reaching over to pat Charley's hand. "I guess she's never seen you dance."

"We wore leotards at first," Charley said quietly, thinking on those days, "and we learned the basics, which seemed to take forever. It seemed boring to her after a few times, so she finally stopped coming to watch us."

"You're coming in?" Charley asked, carefully holding the folder of papers against herself as a sudden gust of wind tried to grab it from her.

"They usually go bowling on Tuesday nights, so maybe I can get these signed while you're here, you can take them with you."

"Yes. That might be best," Anna replied, glancing around the area as she exited the car. "We don't want anything getting lost."

"I didn't think it was supposed to rain again," Charley said, wrapping her jacket around her as the first drops of rain could be felt in the darkening air.

"Me either," Anna said, following Charley up the steps to the front door. "Sometimes these storms seem to come up out of nowhere."

"Oh, damn," Charley said, ducking down as a arcing bolt of lightning raced across the sky with a thunderous clap of noise, the heavy smell of ozone lingering around them.

"I think that hit your house," Anna said, as they raced hand in hand onto the porch.

"Yeah," Charley said, stopping to look out around them at the storm. "It seems to be passing now. That was strange."

"Is everybody alright?" William asked, opening the front door to let them in, "I saw you pull up, and then that lightning strike shook the whole place."

"We're fine, dad," Charley assured him, allowing Anna to enter first. "I told you having lightning rods on the house would come in handy one day."

"I'm beginning to think I should have listened to you more often," William said, exchanging looks with her. "Come on in, make yourself at home," he said, turning to Anna. "We were just about to sit down to eat something, it's Italian night."

"That's a kind offer, Mr. Macintyre, but I'm still on the clock," Anna said, brushing at some of the raindrops on her clothing. "It's best that I continue on. Perhaps another night would be best."

"This is Miss Anna," Charley said, introducing her, as she brought the folder out from beneath her jacket. "She's a lawyer for my new job, and just wanted to witness the signing of some papers."

"Ohh, look at you," Darlene said, coming out of the kitchen.

"I like that outfit on you. What a change."
"Yeah mom, it's mine to keep," Charley said, taking the jacket off her shoulders. "Did Jacob stop by to tell you I'd be late?"
"Yes, dear and I've been on pins and needles ever since," Darlene said, reaching over to take Anna hand in greeting. "You must be the new boss."
"Nice to meet you," Anna said, before bringing out a pen from a pocket. "Actually, I'm just one of the employee's myself. I handle the legal paperwork, and make sure all of our new people are properly set up. I guess I'm the boss's right hand."
"I was just saying to your husband that I wouldn't be able to stay long," looking up as a distant rumble could be heard from the passing storm. "I've got to get these papers processed and filed."

"$3,000 a month, plus a signing bonus. I should have been a model when I was younger," William said, giving a smile to his wife, before glancing back down at the papers.
"Hey, maybe some of this can go towards your college fund," he added, looking up as the thought hit him.
"Sure, dad, I was thinking on that myself," Charley replied, giving Anna a quick glance as William picked up the pen.
"She'll be involved in classes for awhile," Anna said, turning to Darlene. "The proper walk, how to pose for the camera. The company had rented a home on the edge of your neighborhood, and that's where I first saw Charley passing by. I knew she was the look we were after for our European markets when I saw all that deep copper hair she has."
"I'll be out and about until school starts," Charley said, trying to ease any concerns. "Then they might fly me to places

on the weekend for a photo shoot, or fashion openings."

"After your homework is finished," William added, giving Anna a glance before settling his gaze on Charley.

"Of course, dad and I'll have a tutor along with me. It's in there somewhere," nodding towards the papers.

"Oh, so I see," William said, glancing further down the page, "and a chaperone as well. That makes me feel better. All these young kids, getting into drugs and running wild these days," he said, looking up at Anna. "You can't be too careful."

"I agree. The company will have someone at her side," Anna replied, nodding at his words. "We don't condone any mischief or childish attitudes. We're a business, and it's serious work."

"What about your hula lessons, down at the center." Darlene asked, looking over to Charley.

"I think I can still do both," Charley said. "I explained that to Anna on the way here and she's thinking I can afford private lessons if I'm off on an assignment."

"Go ahead and sign, dear," Darlene said, gesturing towards the papers on the counter, "Our girl's going to be rich and famous one day."

"I get to keep some of the clothes I model too," Charley said, giving her mother a smile. "I'll have to go through my closet."

"Well, the best of luck on all this," William said, signing with a flourish. "Don't forget to have someone figure out your taxes, don't end up like those movie stars your mother reads about in those magazines she gets."

"That takes care of the paperwork for now," Anna said, placing the papers back in the folder. "I'll be back in the morning to get her started on her first day."

"That went well," Charley sighed, leaning against the

doorframe as she accompanied Anna to the porch. "They're both clueless on modeling, same as for my dancing. I've never danced the hula."

"Did you know that the British banned the dance back in the 1820's," Charley asked, showing a gleam in her eyes. "Tahitian dancing, I mean. I guess it was too sensual for them, too daring for mere mortal men."

"You are bold," Anna finally said, judging Charley's expression.

"Will I do well?" Charley asked, letting a tired face show.

"You'll be fine, unless she asks you to bring something back in her size," Anna said, showing a smile. "Then we've both got a problem. Ten in the morning, I'll be waiting out here."

"Charley?" Anna said, looking back as she stood on the sidewalk.

"Yes?" Charley replied, leaning forward to hear.

"I enjoyed our talk today. You're much more than I was told," Anna said, giving her a nod. "You're the one."

"Oh, here," she added reaching into a pocket to bring out the car keys. "These stay with you, the paperwork is inside, and don't worry, my ride should be here any minute. I'll meet them up at the corner."

"What are you smiling about?" William asked, noting the expression on Darlene's face as he picked up their bowling ball cases.

"Charley," Darlene said, the smile widening. "She'll have to wear a dress. It just came to me while we were having supper."

"Hey, Mr. Macintyre," Jacob said, sliding up on his bike. "Charley home?"

"Sure, Jacob," William replied, seeing Darlene's smile

reappear again. "In there cleaning up from supper. There's plenty left if you're hungry."

"William, whose car is this," Darlene asked, pointing over to Charley's vehicle. "That girl must have broken down or something."

"Say, Jacob, could you ask Charley about this car here before we leave?" William asked, catching Jacob just before he opened the screen.

"That's mine," Charley called out, opening the door wider for Jacob. "I forgot to mention, it came with the new job. It's in the fine print."

"Wow," Jacob said, walking back over to the edge of the porch to look. "That's a fancy one. Man, just wait until school starts, they'll mob around you."

"No taking off anywhere, Jamie's upstairs," Darlene said, shaking a finger towards Charley, "There's dishes."

"I wasn't planning on going anywhere, mom," Charley sighed, giving Jacob a glance. "Come on, I saved you a plate. You'll find it in the oven."

"What went on after I left, did you have to get naked?" Jacob asked, carefully using some bread to get up the last of the sauce on his plate.

"Yeah, sure did. They took lots of pictures," Charley replied, hiding her smile. "I had to pose on this white bearskin rug, my hair down and wild looking. It really set off my deep copper tones."

"You should learn to cook," Charley said as Jacob sat back in his chair, pushing his plate away from him. "They teach some of that in school, it's held in that class room with all the ovens and girls."

"Bet ya it doesn't taste all that good," Jacob replied, making a face at the notion. "I don't think that's for me."

"Yes, I suppose you right," Charley said, sitting down at the table while she waited to claim the plate from him. "We better not try that, it might not taste good. That's beginning to sound like sour grapes to me."

"Well," Jacob replied, letting out a slight burp. "I don't like them as much as the other kind."

"No, I don't suppose you would," Charley replied, finally snagging the plate from him. "It's a shame you never learned to wash dishes either."

"That's girl's work, everybody knows that," Jacob said, rubbing his stomach. "The guys would laugh at me if they saw me doing that kind of stuff with you."

"Ah... I see," Charley replied, standing up to take the plate over to the sink. "Girls work... like posing in the swimsuits, and smiling all innocent like, while showing off someone's latest versions of hot pants."

"I think the guys over in Europe would wish they were right there in that photograph with me, doing *girl's work* too. Shame it's so different here."

"You were wearing short shorts?" Jacob asked, his eyes going over to Charley's backside, as a mental picture of shorts came to him.

"The shortest," Charley said, hiding her expression from him as she quickly washed the plate. "I suppose reading all the fashion magazines is just girl's work too, you'll miss out when the magazine prints my photographs."

"Well, I don't read them," Jacob said, picking up the other items from the table and bringing them over to the sink for her.

"Oh, I know." Charley sighed, keeping her attention on her washing. "You just look at the pictures, same as everybody else."

Chapter Three

"Morning. How did you sleep," Anna asked, watching Charley take the steps two at a time coming down off the porch.

"Just great, snug as a bug," Charley replied, grinning. "It was like I had someone watching over me all night."

"That's a good choice," Anna added, noting the shorts and sleeveless top Charley had chosen for the day as she opened the car door for her. "You'll want to be comfortable."

"Where we headed?" Charley asked, seeing that they were continuing through the neighborhood.

"You remember the house, the one that had the sign?" Anna asked, giving a quick glance over to Charley before focusing back on the road.

"Sure, who could forget that place," Charley replied, nodding her head at the memory. "There's this huge grotesque or maybe it's a gargoyle I guess, up on the edge of the roof."

"There is?" Anna said, raising an eyebrow. "I don't recall that."

"Well, I don't see how you could have possibly missed it, it was really wicked looking and had these teeth showing," making a face to demonstrate while lifting up both hands as if they were claws. "It'll give you the shivers.

"That thing was impressive."

"He didn't scare you?" Anna asked, as they turned down towards where the house was located.

"Nope, I've seen pictures of them before, I just adore them. I have a little statue of one on a shelf in my room. Somebody must of given it to me when I was little," Charley said, leaning forward in her seat to look up at the roof line of the house as they arrived, almost missing a gate opening for them to reveal a driveway leading in towards the shadowed side of the house.

"I don't see it now," Charley said, looking over to Anna with a hint of confusion on her face. "I know I saw one."

"Maybe it was the other side," Anna replied, gesturing them towards the wide wooden front door before them. "We'll have to take a look later."

"Yeah, maybe it decided to move, to watch the sunrise," Charley said, giving Anna a look as they went up the wide steps to the door. "I know what I saw."

"Hmmm, interesting comment," Anna sighed, opening the door for her and following her into the coolness of the hallway.

"Why's that?" Charley asked, glancing back at Anna, as they entered a neat foyer.

"Because everything is not as what you might think it is," Anna said, leading them down a hallway, before going around the first landing stairs, and towards a room across from the kitchen. "That's one of the lessons for today."

"This is Georgie, and Gretta," Anna said, introducing the two older occupants of the room they entered. "Maybe they can explain what it was that you say you saw."

"Hey," Charley said, waving a hand at the pair who had stood up from the far side of a dark oaken table as she entered.

"Please, come on in, Charley," Gretta said, speaking first, her pleasant voice carrying across the room. "Have a seat here with us."

"Yes," Georgie, said, nodding to an empty chair, "No need to be shy with us, we've got all day to sit and talk. Sometimes, that's all we do," giving Gretta a quick glance. "At my age, the choices are few."

"About gargoyles?" Charley asked, noting their expressions as she slowly set herself down at the end of the table, trying to remember where she had seen them before.

"Gargoyles?" Gretta replied, glancing over at Anna before finding her own chair again, "An odd topic. Why gargoyles, Charley?"

"Oh, I suppose it's partly to do with the fact that I must have see half a dozen of them yesterday, back at the office," Charley replied, leaning back and getting comfortable as she quietly tapped the table top with her new ring. "I actually checked in the mirror when I got up this morning, to see if anyone had tattooed one on my backside while I was sleeping.

"And, upon arrival here, I discovered that the one I saw perched up on the roof the other day isn't anywhere to be found. Anna is trying to make me think I'm seeing things."

"I see," Georgie said, after sharing looks with Gretta. "You think what you saw was real. A real gargoyle."

"Yes, I think what I saw was real," Charley said, nodding her head at the idea. "I didn't say it was alive, just real. You don't have to believe me."

"What's the difference, I mean, they were all different depictions of some creature that surely must have been alive for someone to have an image to carve," Gretta said, keeping her gaze on Charley.

"I saw a statue in the lobby of the office building I was in the other day," Charley said. "It seemed to be to be a very close duplicate of the one I had seen on the roof… but the pose was different. I touched it, so it was really there, therefore gargoyles are real. At this point, that's what I know."

"So... you tell yourself it's real, and it becomes real," Georgie said, leaning forward and placing his hands under his chin as he kept his gaze on Charley. "You shifted reality in your mind to meet your expectations."

"No, it was already real, I simply acknowledged the fact," Charley said, trying to see where the conversation was leading to. "The gargoyle didn't change, at least not while I was looking at it."

"Why didn't you say that the figure was just a copy of a gargoyle, and that piece of stone wasn't actually a real one," Anna asked, getting interested in the conversation.

"As I said," Charley said, giving a slight smile. "Because I touched it... and that gargoyle knew I was there."

"See, I told you she'd know," Gretta suddenly said, reaching out to slap Georgie on one shoulder. "Just like her mother."

"You're putting two and two together." Georgie said, his eyes still on Charley.

"I'm aware that two and two does not always equal four," Charley said, her face changing expression at the mention of her mother, "but I don't know everything."

"Interesting, can you prove that?" Anna asked, displaying her raised eyebrow once more.

"Sure, it's easy," she replied, looking around at them. "Take two drops of water and place them in a cup. If you add two more... you don't have four drops in your cup, you have just one."

"She's got you there," Gretta said, nodding her head, "and she knows that you can now get more than four drops back out, simply by changing the reality... making smaller drops."

"Or just leaving it as one large drop." Georgie added, giving Charley a smile.

"You seem pleased with my ideas on gargoyles," Charley said, looking over to Anna. "Could you explain what this has to do with my mom?"

"Soon," Anna replied, glancing around to Gretta and Georgie, "but it wasn't your mom, it was your *mother*."

"You mean my *real* mother," Charley replied, sitting back to look around at all of them. "You all knew her."

"Yes, we knew her, at least I knew of her," Anna finally said, letting out a deep sigh as she looked down at the table before meeting Charley's eyes. "From what I've been told, you're just like her. Same attitude, same appearance, it's almost as if you were a younger twin."

"Same natural *gifts*?" Charley asked, keeping her gaze on Anna.

"Well, that is an interesting question, isn't it?" Georgie said, leaning forward. "That's what we'd like to find out."

"After lunch," Gretta said, lightly tapping the table with the palms of both hands. "I've got a nice easy meal all planned for us."

"Can I be of any assistance?" Charley asked, grabbing an extra apron from the back of one of the chairs as she followed Gretta into the kitchen.

"Why sure, that'll be a great help," Gretta said, giving her a nod. "I mention kitchen work, and it's just me in here until those smells from the oven reach the living room."

"You really knew my mother?" Charley asked, bringing out the lunch items from the refrigerator and placing them on the counter as Gretta opened the package of paper plates. "I've seen you before, at the Center, with the moms watching us dance. Georgie, I think I've seen him in the grocery store."

"Yes, we've been around you, and we knew her for many

years," Gretta said, pausing for a moment to reflect. "She's right, you're her daughter. That's certain."

"That girl could tell you to go to hell in five languages, and only one that you'd ever recognize," Gretta added, pointing to a loaf of bread for Charley to bring over. "She was a bit touchy at times."

"On edge?" Charley asked, returning to get the mayo out.

"Yes, I guess that a good way to describe her... always thinking on things, the fate of the world I suppose," Gretta said, preparing the sandwiches. "Stubborn too," hiding her smile from Charley, "She could be a handful at times."

"You'll find a pie in the oven, I put it in there earlier," pointing towards the stove with her knife. "You're favorite."

"Blueberry, how did you guess?" Charley asked, savoring the smell as she carried it over to the counter.

"He didn't stop to peek at you, in case you got the wrong idea," Gretta suddenly said, turning and leaning back against the counter to look at Charley. "He misses her, too. He just wanted to check on you. He says you look much nicer with your hair down."

"He? You mean my mysterious watcher that Anna told me about," Charley asked. "She mentioned a 'Senior Partner', is that the one?"

"I suppose that's one way to describe him," Gretta said, showing a smile. "I don't know how *senior* he would be... he mentioned to me that you held a great beauty. He's got great eyesight."

"That tells me a lot," Charley said, showing a frown. "No one has a photo, and everybody talks around him like he's a phantom."

"If he was a ghost, you wouldn't be his ring bearer, now would you, dear?" Gretta said, showing a broad grin, as she brushed a lock of gray hair away from her face. "Let's go call the those hungry souls in, and stand back. They can get in a mad rush some days."

"Gretta, Anna told me there were others with rings." Charley said, pausing before going to the door.

"Yes...but there has always been only one with that image on it," Gretta said, her eyes going to Charley's ring. "It has been handed down, no one outside your family has ever worn it, nor would he accept that."

"This was my mother's?" Charley asked, the surprise showing on her face as she raised her hand to look at the ring again.

"It's yours, now," Gretta said, giving Charley a smile. "Wear it with honor and pride."

"In time, you will notice others coming to you, all will want to greet you, others will come seeking answers to questions that you might hold the answer to," Gretta added, picking up a hand towel to wipe her fingers off. "You'll be treated with great respect. It comes with the job."

"I smell pie," Georgie said, poking his head through the doorway. "Can we eat?"

"See, I told you they'd come asking questions," Gretta said, giving out a light laugh.

"Can't even have the time to get it to the table," Charley said, placing hands on hips as Anna could be seen peering over Georgie's shoulder.

"Someone needs to take charge," Gretta said quietly, nodding to Charley. "They've been a handful since you've been gone."

"What do you mean?" Charley asked, glancing over to Gretta as the others entered and found a place at the kitchen table. "I just got here a little while ago, I haven't been here before."

"Oh, yes you have," Georgie replied, giving a grin. "You were born upstairs in your mother's bed."

"Wait a minute," Charley let out, trying to deal with what had been said. "Whose house is this?"

"It's yours, of course," Anna replied, reaching out for one of the plates. "At least when you turn eighteen. It's in the will, Gretta and Georgie are just keeping an eye on it for you."

"Where's our boy, he loves blueberry." Gretta asked, glancing over towards Georgie.

"He's usual spot, upstairs sitting over top her bedroom as before. Back on the job where he belongs, and announcing to the world that the Lady is in residence."

"Everything in its time." Anna said, noting Charley's expression.

"The gargoyle's back, up on the roof," Charley asked, looked around the table. "Right?"

"Tell me something," Anna asked, leaning back and looking over at Charley. "What is a gargoyle?"

"Well, I think there are several ideas on that going around," Charley said as Gretta began serving slices of pie. "The word is French, so you might have some insight on that."

"I'm interested in what you think they are, the word itself is thought to come from the word *throat,* as they were used to channel the water off the roofs of buildings."

"Such as old churches," Charley said, nodding her head while picking up her fork. "I've read that, but it doesn't really explain why they look the way they do.

"I think they're something really old, and very Pagan," Charley added, seeing Gretta was about to ask a question. "I don't know where they came from, but I've always thought that they ward off evil… provide some sort of protection for those unable to defend themselves."

"How they got involved with the early church is still a mystery to me, but that's where you'd find most of them these days, at least the copies, the ones carved from stone."

"You say protect those who are unable to help themselves," Georgie said, scrapping the last of his pie up. "Doesn't that indicate some form of morality at work, and perhaps a higher intelligence?"

"Yes, I suppose it could," Charley said, sitting back in her seat. "It just tells me there is more to the story. I just haven't figured it all out yet."

"You seem open to the idea that there's more, a lot more to the story," Gretta said, exchanging glances with Anna.

"Well, blame Anna. She was the one who told me today's lesson was on what's real," Charley responded with, showing a little grin. "I don't have an issue with dropping my misunderstanding's. I understand what's left, strange as it might be, is the truth."

"What are your thoughts on evil," Anna asked. "You said the gargoyles warded it away. Do you think it's some dark force in the universe?"

"You mean like some sort of fog bank?" Charley asked. "No, I don't think so. I think it's inside us, and we choose whether or not to release it. It's people that are evil, and maybe those gargoyles are speaking to that element within us, that part that inherently knows what is good and what is bad."

"I think you define it by looking at the intentions of others, that tells me what I want to know. I understand an accident is simply the result of natural events coming together, cause and effect. The evil is in the driver who decides to run down the kid on the bike that's been annoying him for the last month."

"Interesting," Anna mused, keeping her eyes on Charley. "In that case, do you think the driver should be punished for his actions?"

"Sure, if the system works and he's caught. Good luck on proving that in court if nobody witnessed it," giving out a little sigh. "Possession by evil your Honor, it won't happen again, I promise. Can I go home now?"

"Ultimately, we should be held accountable. The innocent shouldn't have to endure the wrath of others who are stronger, or have some power over them. The balance should be restored when such actions are discovered."

"How do you know what is evil, and what is just a lapse in judgment?" Gretta asked, keeping her eyes on her.

"I think you know evil when you see it." Charley said, pushing her empty plate away from her on the table.

"Do you, know it when you see it?" Gretta asked, sharing another glance with the others.

"One of my natural gifts," Charley sighed. "Not perfect, I have my off days, but I think I do."

"Your mother had such gifts," Gretta said, thinking on her words.

"Aren't we getting ahead of ourselves?" Georgie asked, giving Gretta a quick look.

"She needs to know," Anna said, showing a slight frown. "*We* need to know."

"Know what?" Charley asked, giving them a questioning look. "I've always known I had a natural gift as you call it."

"You don't know the half of it," Gretta said. "Maybe we should start there and see where that takes us."

"We could all end up in a dimensional jump," Georgie said, pursing his lips at the idea. "We'll need him, too."

"You mean Jake?" Charley asked, looking to Anna.

"Who is Jake?" Gretta asked, glancing to the others.

"Beats me, I just decided to give him a name since no one else has. How's it feel to have a name with no body?" Charley said. "I'm thinking it's pretty much like having no body with no name to go with it," sitting back and crossing her arms in front of her, waiting on a reply.

"It's not Jake, I can at least tell you that," Anna said, a smile coming to her face.

"Here," Georgie said, reaching out to slide the remaining half of the pie closer to Charley. "How about we let you discover that for yourself."

"How about we put a couple of paper plates under that first," Gretta said, reaching for the pie. "It'll get bent up, just like the last one. I'm not getting a discount by buying them a dozen at a time."

"What?" Charley asked, looking around at the expectant faces as the pie was transferred.

"Top floor, there's a door that leads to the attic. From there you can get out onto the roof, if that's where he is," Gretta said, nodding down at the pie. "Take that with you."

"He won't need a fork, he likes to use his hands a lot," Anna said quietly, her eyes on Charley. "Of course, you could feed it to him, less mess."

"He'd like that," Gretta said, giving Charley a smile.

"No doubt," Charley said, carefully lifting the plate. "All the way up the stairs?" she asked, beginning to feel a little nervous.

"And through the door." Anna added, pointing towards the hallway.

"Oh crap," Charley muttered to herself, standing at the bottom of the steps for the first floor and peering upwards towards the top. "It's dark up there."

"This is just another one of their tests," she said, keeping her voice low as she made her way up. "There's probably a kangaroo or something penned up there. A wild animal, something scary that jumps out at you."

"Probably a bunch of bats that's taken over the attic… fruit bats," thinking of the blueberries. "Yeah, fruit bats. That's got to be it," taking another step upwards.

"I haven't heard a scream yet." Georgie said, looking over to Gretta and Anna.

"She hasn't had time to get to the attic yet," Anna replied, shifting in her seat to hear any sounds coming down the stairs. "I don't think she's the screaming type."

"You might want to go and find the antidote," Gretta finally said after another minute of silence. "She might make it all the way."

"Man, all this for a lousy quarter mil a year," Charley said, pausing to admire the grandfather clock standing against the wall on the second floor landing, giving out a little jump as it suddenly began to chime the hour.

"Maybe she's fainted," Georgie said, looking over to Gretta. "Now I'm going to have to carry her back down. I'm getting too old for this line of work."

"He'd have her down here if that had happened," Gretta said, giving him a look. "Wait. She's about to discover the truth."

"Well, she better not faint, that's all I'm saying. Did you remember to bake a second pie this time," Georgie muttered, looking around the kitchen with a hopeful expression.

Balancing the plate on one palm, Charley gingerly turned the handle on the door, allowing it to swing wide open before her with a low creaking noise.

"Hello?" Charley let out, slowly realizing that she had only spoken in a whisper. "Anyone in here?" she asked, forcing herself to speak a little louder as she peered into the room, using the dim light from the hall.

"You may place it on the table, there," a voice said, causing Charley to quickly look around at the dark shadows.

"Wait a minute, I didn't hear that," Charley said, taking a few small steps into the room until she noticed the table. "That was inside my head."

"Very perceptive," the deep voice said. "I don't speak very well."

"Where are you?" Charley asked leaning over, trying to spot the speaker in the gloom of the attic, noting the creaks from the thick oak timbered flooring as the shadow moved closer, causing her to stumble back against the table.

"Here, little Lady," sounded in her mind as two large hands suddenly grasped her beneath each arm as she set the pie down, lifting her up effortlessly until her feet were left dangling several feet off the floor. "Welcome home."

"Your hands are warm... I think... I think I'm going to be sick," was all Charley could say as she found herself facing a pair of ruby red eyes that seemed glow with an inner light as a face emerged from the darkness and a pleasantly scented odor enveloped her.

"Oh damn, I'm going to fall," Charley let out as she finally opened her eyes at the breeze and sunlight on her face, clutching at the arm she felt around her waist.

"I thought you would enjoy the view," the voice said. "The roof is flat here on the section that faces the rear of the house. There is always a nice breeze."

"We're up on top of the third floor!" Charley exclaimed, her eyes widening as she realized her situation, trying to scoot backwards away from the edge, her shoes sliding helplessly on the smooth tiles.

"Nice spot," the voice said, using a soothing tone as a quick wind came around the corner, causing Charley to tighten her grip on the arm as she realized she was being held from behind, the warmth of his body penetrating her clothing, and there was no place to go.

"I can take you to the edge if you still feel you're going to be ill," the voice said, the perception of a grin lingering with the comment as the arm around her waist loosened slightly.

"No, no… I'm doing much better," Charley let out, grabbing at the arm again as another gust of wind pushed against her. "Maybe we should go back inside now."

"You might want to rest first, get your heartbeat lower," the voice advised. "The way back inside is up above you."

"What?" Charley said, twisting herself around, and looking up over her shoulder to the attic. "I've got to climb back?"

"Going down is quicker," the voice advised, his grip loosening a little more.

"Be nice," Charley said, trying to control herself, "I brought you pie… some blueberry."

Suddenly, without warning, Charley felt the hands grabbing her again. Struggling as he lifted her once more as she arced back, her hair flowing freely around her as her sudden cry was lost to the winds that surrounded her.

For a brief second, everything lost focus, and then she felt the welcoming wooden floor of the attic beneath her feet as she collapsed down on it, landing face first beside the small table with a gasp. The last image she saw before fainting was that of a large dark shadow coming in through the shuttered window towards her.

"You are in so much trouble," Gretta said, placing her hands on her hips as she faced the darkness in the corner of the attic "You know damn well she's under the effects of the inhibitor."

"That didn't seem to concern her very much," the voice replied, a light tone of remorse showing in his words, "She shifted back inside on her own. I was going to bring her back inside, how was I to know?"

"I wouldn't give a plugged nickel for your ass right now, boy," Georgie muttered, glancing over as he helped Anna to get a dizzy Charley upright "If I were you, I'd be looking for a better place to hide. She's going to put your butt in the hospital when she come back up here."

"It wasn't my fault. I was about to return her, she promised me pie," the voice replied, his uncertainty showing "What can I do?"

"I'd suggest you sit down and eat your pie," Gretta told him, shaking her head "I hope it tastes good after all this, because she's not likely to bring you another any time soon."

"I suggest you run away from home," Anna said, taking one side as Georgie took the other and they led Charley towards the stairs.

"The guest room up here will do." Anna said, guiding the trio along the length of the banister.

"Oh, I don't feel so good." Charley moaned, trying to hold her head still as she was placed on a large soft bed.

"We'll need the flask, and a glass," Anna said, looking to Georgie. "I wasn't expecting this for at least a month."

"I was hoping to be retired," Georgie replied, shaking his head as he left to find the items Anna asked for.

"Don't you worry, dear," Gretta said, placing a pillow behind Charley's head. "We've got something special coming to take care of that headache, and the dizziness as well. Just try to close your eyes and relax. That'll help."

"Maybe I should go home," Charley said, closing her eyes as a wave of nausea swept over her again.

"You are home," Gretta said, trying to give a soothing tone to her words as she fussed with Charley's hair. "You used to play in here, you know. Many's the time I had to crawl under this very bed to find you."

"Hurry up, you old geezer," Gretta suddenly yelled out, trying to make herself heard downstairs.

"I'm on my way, don't have kittens up there," Georgie muttered, as he made his way up to the landing. "I don't have wings ya know."

"What's that?" Anna asked looking up at the sound coming from the attic.

"Damn," Georgie said, making his way into the room, setting the needed items down next to the bed before looking over to Gretta. "He hasn't done that in nearly twenty years."

"Oh, that sounds so sad." Charley said, slowly turning her head to listen. "It makes me want to cry too."

"His wail of lament," Gretta said. "That's a rare thing to hear."

"Pay him no mind," Anna said. "You'll be able to deal with that one later."

"What's happening to me?" Charley asked, as another wave of dizziness engulfed her. "I thought I was going to be a super spy. I don't understand what's going on. I feel so weak."

"Super spy?" Georgie asked quietly, giving Anna a look as he crossed his arms and leaned back against the doorframe to be out of the way.

"I had to put it in a way she understood, that's all," Anna explained while giving a slight shrug. "That was the only thing that came up in our conversation."

"What was I to say," Anna continued, noting Georgie's expression. "She's a Phase Shifter… one of the Guardians?"

"Well, that closer to the truth of it," he replied letting out a sigh as he looked at Charley and then Gretta. "It's time you released her."

"Charley," Gretta began, sitting down on the edge of the bed. "Listen, I've got something to tell you, about why you're feeling so bad."

"You have more than one special gift, as you call it, and when you were very young, before you were adopted, you were given something to nullify them."

"A magic potion?" Charley asked, narrowing her eyes at the thought.

"Just like in them fairy tales," Georgie muttered, "It was to protect you until you were old enough to understand."

"The flask holds the cure," Anna said, standing on the other side of the bed. "When you got scared, out on the roof, you shifted back inside because you thought you were going to fall. You knew the attic was a safe place. That wasn't supposed to happen. His presence seems to have triggered something within you."

"What's this stuff again?" Charley asked, giving the dusty flask a dubious look.

"Antidote," Gretta said, giving a nod towards the drink.

"Wizard's juice," Georgie said, looking over at the small flask as Gretta wiped it off. "It's good for what ails you. I think it's aged long enough," giving Gretta a glance.

"What, I was cursed as a child?" Charley asked, trying not to groan as she looked over to Gretta, as a glass of deep blue liquid was poured. "I'm sick?"

"No, it more like being out of balance with yourself." Anna said, trying to explain.

"You mean like with hormones," Charley replied, closing her eyes for a moment.

"Yeah, that's a good one to use," Georgie said wryly,

nodding his head, "but, it's not really yourself that you're out of balance with, it's the rest of the universe."

"Here," Gretta said picking up the glass and holding it for Charley to take a sip. "Drink this, and all will be better."

"Does it taste nasty?" Charley asked, before lifting a shaky hand up to take the glass.

"It's going to taste like blueberries," Gretta explained, giving Georgie a stern glance at the expression on his face. "She's just a child."

"She won't be once she drinks that," Georgie replied, using a low voice as he watched Charley.

"Pay that old fool no mind," Gretta said, returning her attention to Charley. "He's gotten old and set in his ways and attitudes of late. This is what you need, so bottoms up."

"Oh, this tastes good." Charley exclaimed, her eyes widening as she took a tentative sip and then quickly drank the remainder.

"I don't see any smoke coming from her ears," Georgie noted after a moment, as they all waited to see a reaction.

"She still out?" Anna asked, pausing in her pacing in the hall beside the banister.

"Not by much," Georgie replied, still lounging against the doorframe. "She's mumbling something, looks a bit flushed to me."

"He's stopped his wail, it's too darn quiet up there," Anna added, looking towards the attic door.

"Yeah, he knows what's up," Georgie said, following her glance. "He's probably wondering what's going to happen to his butt next. I'm surprised he hasn't tried to creep down here to her room."

"He wouldn't fit though the door," Anna muttered, looking

into the room at Charley.

"You seen them bats get themselves into those tiny cracks and crevices haven't you?" Georgie asked, turning to look at her. "Just like a bat, he'd be in here, all quiet and sneaky. Trying to hide in the closet or something, maybe get underneath the bed. They're the reason kids are afraid to sleep with an arm hanging down the side of the bed at night."

"You and your tales," Gretta sighed, giving Georgie a glance. "I don't which of the two of you is worse."

"Well, at least I didn't take night classes to be a witch doctor," Georgie responded, sharing a grin with Anna. "You should tell your patient there about how they make you dance naked under the full moon."

"Who's dancing naked?" Charley asked, slowing sitting while holding the cool cloth Gretta had placed on her forehead.

"I guess you've still got the touch, she's alive," Georgie noted as Charley swung her feet around to the edge of the bed and sat up.

"Oh boy, the world's not spinning around anymore. My head feels like I'm almost back to normal." Charley let out while dropping the cloth she had been holding down to her lap.

"I've used the time off to notice you grumble a lot," Charley said, giving Georgie a look, before looking over to Anna. "Where's he hiding?"

"Up in the dark," Gretta said, reaching out to take the cloth. "You might want to sit there for a spell, just to make sure you won't fall over when you stand up."

"I'll deal with it," Charley said, standing up and looking around the room to check her balance. "I'm all better. The magick worked."

"What's his real name?" Charley asked, looking over to

Georgie. "So when I scream at him, he'll know whom I'm talking too."

"In ancient India he was known as *Bitsok*, one who does not morn. Where they spoke Latin, they called him *Nex*. It means violent death, and sometimes they used the term *mortifera*, whenever the thought of deadly things came up that they couldn't understand," Georgie said, keeping his eyes on Charley. "A more modern concept is the Reaper, but I think he'll answer to whatever name you use up there. He'll grovel for blueberry pie."

"I've called him Jaradan over these many years," Gretta said, "but Georgie is right, he'll listen to whatever name you choose. You bear his ring."

"Ancient India, he's been around that long?" Charley asked, looking over to Georgie, thinking on what he had said.

"Since before that, long time before that," Georgie replied, giving out a little sigh. "No one can tell you his age, expect maybe himself. I've never found the opportunity to ask you understand. Like with the tigers at the zoo, I don't stand that close, nor do I ask questions."

"What I can tell you, is that your ring is just as old as he is," Georgie added.

Chapter Four

"Oh, I didn't notice those before," Charley exclaimed, noticing the soft glow against the far wall as she entered the attic.

"Her stone collection," Jaradan said. "She picked them up from place to place, said she liked the way they shone whenever she walked by."

"They're all some kind of crystals, large ones," Charley said quietly, watching as the glow increased as she walked over to the shelf. "So many different colors, it's like a rainbow of light in here now."

"How come they didn't light up like this the first time I came in here." she asked after a moment, reaching out to tap one of the crystals with a finger before turning to face the darkness in the far corner.

"We have much to discuss, you and I," he said, stepping closer to the light, his height sending shadows against the walls as he moved.

"Oh, boy," was all Charley got out as she stared up at him, his muscles standing out beneath his skin like steel cables as he shifted his weight, his wide wings arcing back as he positioned himself before her.

Keeping her eyes on him, she examined his face, it's almost

fox like shape, until one saw the teeth set below his ruby red eyes, eyes that returned her look with an unflinching gaze.

"I saved the pie, we should sit down and share it together," he said, the words rolling around in her mind as she continued to be amazed by the sight before her. "You'll get a stiff neck looking up all the time."

"Retractable claws," Charley said, checking his hands. "That's why I didn't get sliced into ribbons when you grabbed me."

"Oh, ah..." she suddenly let out, raising a hand to one eyebrow as she studied the floor for a moment, "You're covered with a fine fur... and... you're naked."

"Clothing is a human concept. I've done well with the feel of nature against my skin," Jaradan replied, the smile evident in his tone. "You should try it more often yourself. It seems to suit you."

"You thought we looked like those statues on the churches," he added, seeing her expression. "Like those dolls you humans sell in your stores for children, the ones who are neither male or female because you've accepted the idea that you were born tainted, that your very form is obscene. This game you play angers me, as anyone can see that it is the cause of many problems in your society."

"Opinionated, too," Charley said, taking a step back to look at him. "Don't be so hasty to group me with everybody else. It just caught me by surprise, that's all. I've been to the zoo more than once."

"Tell me, young one," Jaradan said, lowering himself to settle down in front of her. "I understand you study your native tribes in school. Can you tell me what the one called Pocahontas wore?"

"Sure, she wore those deer skin clothes, animal hides. It's

in all the books," Charley replied, "Why?"

"Because the summer temperatures where she lived could reach 90 degrees or greater on any given day. Tell me, how long do you think she wore those animal hides?" he asked, keeping his eyes on her.

"I never looked at that way before, they don't tell you that part in school," Charley said, thinking on what he was saying. "If it were me, I wouldn't even bother to wear them at all, you'd have a heat stoke."

"Oh, wait a minute here," Charley said, sitting down and crossing her legs. "You're the teacher, too."

"You're bright, same as your mother," he replied, pausing to reach out to set the pie down in front of them. "You'll learn to look behind the images you've been raised with, to see the reality that's hidden. None of those native girls wrapped themselves in those animal skins during the summer months. They wore loincloths, same as everyone else. If you knew the truth, everyone would know it was just a natural aspect of their lifestyle, not something that had to be hidden. Your culture is full of such conflicts, it keeps you from doing what seems natural."

"The truth?" Charley asked, watching as the pie was separated into two sections, one large, and one small, with the use of an extended razor sharp claw. "I'm beginning to understand the Englishmen's fascination with Indian maidens, now that I think on that."

"The truth can be a matter of perspective," he said quietly, leaning lower to savor the smell of the pie. "You'll see what I mean as we go along."

"I see," Charley said, watching his response to the blueberries with interest. "You should have given yourself a larger piece," gesturing towards the smaller of the two sections of pie.

"I like a challenge, life around here has been so very dull," he replied, carefully reaching out and snatching the larger section with practiced ease. "By the way, I'm sorry about the roof incident, your return overwhelmed me."

"Yeah, I heard... from the room they had to put me in," Charley said, her tone lowering as she watched in surprise as the entire thing was tossed into his mouth.

"I'm glad to see you're feeling better," he said, licking his lips, "Are you going to eat that?" looking over at Charley's slice of pie.

"No, I'll have supper waiting for me when I get back," Charley said, noting that his hand never paused in reaching out for the rest of the pie. "Help yourself to it," barely making it past her lips before the last piece had followed the first.

"Tell me something, pie lover," Charley asked, "Why on earth did they call ever you *Nex*?"

"Tell me," he finally said, giving out a slight burp, "Given the choice, would you want to find the evil that lurks in the darkest of shadows... or be the one who kills it?"

"Ah, I'm thinking I'd rather be the one doing the pointing," Charley said, her eyes on his. "I'm not exactly designed to do much else."

"You'd be surprised," he finally said, giving her another appraisal with his eyes, "but now you understand our basic positions on the team, for the time being."

"How come Georgie won't get too close to you?" she asked, thinking on what had been told to her.

"Ever see the result of a gargoyle attack?" Jaradan asked, resting himself lower against the floor with a deep rumble from his throat.

"No. Until now, I never really considered it," Charley said, her eyes widening slightly.

"Georgie has, that's why."

"You're the ring bearer," he added, turning his head to keep an eye on her. "If you weren't, you're insecurities would start to come out, you'd feel uncomfortable if I was near."

"Sort of like my dad whenever he sees a cop on the highway, he goes paranoid thinking he's going to get a ticket," Charley said, beginning to relax in his presence.

"Yes, that's a good example," he sighed. "Their fears begin to emerge, and they think something is after them because of the things they've done."

"I thought you were supposed to ward off evil," Charley said, picking up the shredded paper plates and setting them aside.

"Oh, I keep it away in a manner of speaking. I'm your protector, too," he said quietly, gauging her reaction.

"Oh… everything is beginning to come into focus now," Charley said thoughtfully, nodding her head at the revelation. "The evil ones don't just flee, hoping to avoid their fate, they have no qualms in holding their ground and trying to destroy the source of their own fears. Even evil fights for its continued existence."

"That didn't take long for you to figure out. We'll discuss that aspect in greater detail when you return tomorrow," he sighed, giving the doorway a glance. "Anna thinks you've had enough for one day, she's on her way up the stairs. You might want to use your mother's cloak now, it's hanging there at the far end of the shelf."

"Why, is it raining again outside?" Charley asked, standing up to locate it, noting it's sudden comfort as she spread it around her shoulders. "Whoa, the lights just dimmed," she said, glancing at the crystals as they suddenly lost their glow.

"It blocks you, the energy you emit," he explained, idly

watching as Charley held the cloak away from her to see the glow return. "Evil knows when you're around, some more so than others."

"This is wild," Charley said, placing it around her again, seeing the darkness come closer as she lifted the hood to cover her head, taking in the soft scent it held.

"You didn't need that bra, did you," she asked, turning to give him her full attention.

"No. Tell Anna something in a serious tone and she believes every word," Jaradan said, his face displaying a slight smile. "I just wanted to see if you'd do it. I can see you in the dark without any problem. It's waiting for you downstairs by the front door, untouched."

"Oh, just what I need, a nine foot tall killer gargoyle with a warped sense of humor. We're going to have to discuss some thing's when I get back," Charley said, pointing her finger and shaking it as a call was heard outside the door. "Just you wait."

"I'll be here. Waiting is what I do best my Lady," he sighed, his eyes slowly closing as he watched Charley put the cloak around her again, lifting her mane of hair to allowing it to flow down the back and shoulders. "I'm glad you're finally here. The Lady is home."

"I got the message you were on your way," Charley said, smiling at Anna as they met at the landing. "I've learned plenty for one day."

"Oh, don't you look nice," Anna exclaimed, her eyes widening at the sight of the cloak, "You'll have to show Gretta and Georgie, they've been waiting with baited breath down there, wondering how your meeting went."

"Damn." Georgie said, standing up and taking in Charley's appearance.

"Did you tell her?" Greta asked looking from Charley over to Anna.

"No, I thought you would want too," Anna replied. "I was sure surprised."

"Come on, dear," Gretta said, linking arms with Charley. "There's something you might be interested in seeing," as she led them down a hall towards the living room.

"That's me," Charley let out, stopping in front of the large portrait hanging over the huge fireplace mantle, her eyes taking in the deep copper tresses that tried in vain to hide part of the face, as one hand held the grey cloak clutched around her.

"No, that's your mother, Aileana," Gretta said softly. "The former Lady of the house."

"That's my middle name. Do you know where my first name came from?" Charley asked, still engrossed in the painting.

"A book, some story she had been reading, I think," Gretta said, looking back at Charley. "I don't recall the name now."

"Oh, after the heroine maybe, a Southern Belle," Charley mused, glancing over to Gretta with questioning look.

"No, it was a spider as I recall it," Georgie replied, giving her a glance before peering up at the painting again.

"A spider? I'm named after a *spider*?" Charley let out, looking back up at her mother's image. "Why on earth would someone do that?"

"Beats me," Georgie said, shaking his head. "Maybe she was thinking of a Black Widow."

"Hey, there's Walsh," Charley said, pointing him out as they slowly drove past the park. "He's still wearing pants I see."

"That's Jeffery with him," she added as the two boys

stopped to watch the car go past, "Looks like they're up to no good."

"A feeling?" Anna asked, giving the pair a quick glance.

"Maybe, but its subtle. They're probably up to some mischief," Charley mused, "Probably want to break into the school and take a dunk in the pool. Somebody did that a few weeks back and really messed it up. They threw rolls of toilet paper in it on the way out."

"Oh, that wasn't a nice thing to do," Charley said, turning to look back at them. "I recognized that gesture he made when he saw it was me in here."

"You might want to mention that to your new friend in the attic," Anna said, glancing over for a moment. "I'm sure he's full of ideas on how to deal with such things."

"He's full of something alright," Charley said, showing a grin. "The rest of that pie I took up there is only part of it. He's got a serious blueberry addiction."

"Well, I'm sure he means well." Anna said, "I see you got the envelope back."

"Yeah, he left it for me, and I grabbed it on the way out," Charley said, tapping the envelope on her lap. "He's full of surprises too… and he mentioned evil would now know when I was near…" looking back behind them thoughtfully.

"Hey mom, I'm back," Charley called out, going up the stairs.

"I'm in here trying to make some sense of this mess he's made. Mrs. Jamison called. Her kids are needing a babysitter tomorrow," Darlene replied, sticking her head around the doorframe of Jamie's room. "I told her you were busy with a new job, but that I'd let you know."

"Mrs. Jamison, and her brats can find the next poor kid

that's looking for some extra income," Charley muttered, closing her bedroom door behind her with the swing of one foot. "I'm finally free from that."

"Oh, my poor lonesome Teddy," she said, reaching out to poke the bear. "What a sad face we have today. I had a strange day, very strange," dropping the cloak and sitting down on the bed. "I actually saw my mother, a picture at least. Man, let me tell you, she was a fox."

"So was the one up in the attic," she mused, thinking back on his appearance, the warm scent and rippling muscles. "Fox like, I mean," giving the bear another look. "The shape of his head was different than what I was expecting to see close up. He's a little scary looking, but isn't some squat looking monster like you see in the movies, Teddy. He's going to be a handful, that's for sure. I can't explain why, but I liked him right away."

"You're on your own again tomorrow, but I'm driving myself," she said, patting the bear on top of its head.

"I can finally get rid of that ancient computer," she mused, looking around the room at her belongings, "and that TV. Maybe I'll donate them," trying to think of ways to make improvements.

"Actually, it won't be that long before I move out all together," thinking on the third floor bedroom. "I might as well get something set up for myself over there. After all, they told me it was my house."

"I smell mac and cheese, Teddy. Must be that time," Charley said, standing back up. "It'll be fish sticks in about five more minutes, carbon sticks in ten."

"How did your first day go?" Darlene asked, using a towel to set a hot platter of fish down on the table. "Did you get some more clothes?"

"No, well a cloak. I'm just starting out, so it's learning this and learning that," Charley replied, finding her seat. "I was thinking of making some more space in my room up there, dad," looking over to her father. "My TV is up for grabs. You can toss that old thing you have out in the garage, the one that you've been wanting to get fixed for the last two years."

"Oh, that would be nice," Darlene came out with, looking over to William. "You can set the one that works on top on the one that doesn't. Perfect for those games you like to watch on the weekends."

"I'm upgrading my computer later, too, so you might want to consider setting it up for you-know-who," Charley added, rolling her eyes towards Jamie. "I'll be able to afford something new for when school starts back up."

"You know," William said, giving Darlene a quick glance, before looking at Charley, "If you were willing to contribute something to the family budget from your new job, we can get that cable system installed like you always wanted. We got the latest package deal offer in the mail yesterday."

"I see," Charley said, looking at one then the other. "Tell you what, dad. You guys figure out how to get my TV and computer to disappear from my room this week, and I'll pay for the entire installation."

"Sports channel, too?" William asked, surprised by the offer.

"Sure, the works," Charley said, nodding her head. "I'll have something to put towards the budget, too. Of course, that ancient floor model we have out in the living room won't do for the new HD movies. We'll have to go shopping for something better. One of those flat ones that goes on the wall."

"You know," William came out with, after chasing down the last piece of macaroni on his plate, "the Super Store is open till nine," looking up at Charley. "If I call to order the cable in the morning, they'll be expecting to find something to connect it to when they arrive."

"No problem, Dad. I think my signing bonus will cover it," Charley said, sitting back in her chair. "I'll drive us. We can have it delivered and installed as well."

"Sounds like a plan," William said standing up and dropping his napkin. "I can get part of the work done tonight, before we go."

"What's that?" Darlene asked, setting more fish on Jamie's plate.

"Her old computer, it comes apart, so I'll just open the window up there and let gravity take care of the rest. I can toss it all in the trash before I go to bed."

"How come Jamie's being so quiet?" Charley asked, looking over at him as her father left to head upstairs. "He sick?"

"No dear, your father had a talk with him in the den earlier, before you got back. He's learned a lesson on what's proper to say," Darlene said, looking over at Jamie, who only looked over and nodded his head.

"Boy, I never realized shopping could take so much out of you, Teddy," Charley let out, tossing her clothes as she got ready for bed. "Mom went straight to these nice 20 inches display models, and dad and I went to the 50 inch HD plasmas. I got to vote, so we're getting the big one. I ended up getting the smaller one for their room since we're getting the placed wired up."

Resisting the urge to take a peak under the bed, thinking back on what she had overheard Georgie say, she turned off the lamp beside the bed. Reaching down, she grabbed at the cloak she had laid at the end of the bed. Spreading it over her as she laid back down, she let her dreams take over. The attic came to her as a sudden chill caused her to reach out to pull the cloak higher, settling back down as she felt the warmth around her, never noticing the faint glow of the crystals as an arm held her close, and a lowered wing slowly covered her as she fell into a deep untroubled sleep.

"Oh man, I'm so screwed," Charley gasped, trying to determine her whereabouts as she held the cloak tightly against herself. "Where the hell am I, and how did I get here?" she asked looking around the attic. "Where are my clothes?"

"You're home," the voice replied, not bothering to hide the bit of a laugh. "You're wearing your clothes, at least that's all you brought to wear."

"What?" Charley called out, turning, and looking around the room to locate him. "I went to sleep in my own bed. Can somebody *please* tell me what's going on here?"

"You shifted," Gretta said as she entered the attic with a cardboard box in her hands. "Here, try some of these on, they were your mother's."

"I'll take that," Gretta said, as Georgie started to enter behind her with another box. "The poor girl needs some alone time in here, which means you aren't going to be in here gawking while she finds something proper to wear."

"Who gawks?" Georgie replied, trying to peer around the side of the door. "I prefer the slow look of appreciation."

"She'll get someone to drop you out on the roof, you can appreciate all the nature you want from out there," Gretta said, pushing him towards the landing. "Now, take a hike."

"I brought that quilt in earlier for you to spread over her, not to place under her," Gretta fumed, dropping the box next to Charley. "If you want something done right around here, you have to do it yourself."

"She pulled it off, too warm," Jaradan replied. "I thought it softer than the floor. I even folded it over to make it thicker. In here, the Lady chooses," his tone lowering a little to make his point known.

"I hear you," Gretta let out, holding up a hand, before turning her attention to Charley, "Something like this was expected, but it's going faster than I thought it would. Go ahead and choose something from these," reaching down and opening the closest box. "I think you find something that fits, until we can get you back for you own things."

"How did I get here?" Charley asked, giving up on holding the cloak as she pulling out several tops from the box, before looking over to Jaradan.

"You thought yourself here, that's the easiest way to say it," he replied, moving closer. "The attic was in your mind from yesterday, so this is where you ended up."

"You're saying I can go wherever I think of," Charley said, thinking on his answer. "Its a good thing I didn't end up on my front lawn."

"I wouldn't have expected that," Jaradan replied, watching as she rummaged through the box again. "You mother said it was easy, and in the beginning she would count backwards from five while keeping the destination in mind. She said there was a feeling of letting go. You need a memory, or picture to use. You just can't go *nowhere*, there are limitations."

"That's what you guys were talking about the other day, the nullifier potion, or whatever it was I drank." Charley said, sitting back down on the quilt.

"Yes, it blocked certain aspects of yourself. We had hoped it would hold until you were older," Gretta explained, raising an eyebrow at the delay in choosing from the clothing.

"Try it," Jaradan said in her mind. "See the bedroom you were in yesterday. Don't say anything out loud, I can hear you just fine."

"Okay, I'm thinking of the room, the bed and where everything was located." Charley finally gave out, sitting still with her eyes closed.

"See yourself sitting on the bed, same as the last time you were in there, and slowly count backwards with the image firmly set in your mind."

"I don't feel anything working." Charley let out with an exasperated sigh, opening her eyes to see the bedroom walls before her.

"Now you've done it," Gretta let out, seeing the glow forming as Charley winked out with a glimmer in the air. "She's still naked."

"Hey," Charley called out from down the hall, "It worked! How do I get it to work on my clothes?"

"You don't. You go naked," the gargoyle replied, holding up a finger when Gretta opened her mouth to say something.

"What?" Charley asked, her eyes widening as she suddenly reappeared back where she had been sitting.

"I thought that'd get you back here," Jaradan said, nodding his approval at her accomplishment. "Training you is going to be easy."

"You create a kind of self image, so if you're dressed, everything goes with you," Gretta said, shaking her head at Jaradan. "More importantly, anything you're carrying or touching goes, too."

"You mean like another person," Charley said thoughtfully, looking up at the gargoyle, "The bigger picture is beginning to come into focus."

"Anna told me I'd find them, and you'd pull the plug," Charley said, keeping her eyes on the gargoyle. "I'm thinking you'll be pulling their plug permanently."

"I have sworn that the cries of the wicked will be heard louder than the innocents they've destroyed," Jaradan said, slowly nodding his head to Charley. "A little more practice and we'll go hunting, somewhere where evil lurks. Let them tremble at our coming."

"I just got a good idea on where to find some minor evil, but we'll have to wait until later," Charley said, nodding her own head at the idea. "Since I've been there before, it should be a easy journey."

"Well, I suggest you spend a few minutes of the time between to get back and collect a few things of your own to wear," Gretta said, placing hands on hips. "You'll catch cold going like that."

"Oh, I don't know, Gretta," Charley replied, giving herself a glance. "We might go swimming later, and the weather's going to be warm."

"Oh, not you too," Gretta sighed, looking over from Charley to the gargoyle, who just raised both hands up in a shrug of his massive shoulders as he leaned back on his haunches.

"Don't look at me, I wasn't the one who gave her the potion," Jaradan muttered, showing a slight smile. "Maybe it's just her nature, she does have that natural sensuous movement to her form as she walks."

"I give up," Gretta said, shaking her head, "Breakfast in thirty minutes, you might to put something on to keep Georgie from have a anxiety attack every time he looks up from his bacon and eggs. You'll have him seeing double."

"He won't need glasses, that's for sure," Jaradan added, giving Charley a wink as he settled himself back down.

"You're going to end up looking just like your mother."

"You're feeling something, I know that expression," Jaradan said, as Charley paused in putting one shoe on and stared off into space.

"Yeah," she finally let out, finishing with her shoe before pausing again to look at the gargoyle. "It's like the feelings I got before, but amplified, and there's a subtle change. It's as if I would know the source on an individual basis. Its almost like I know the fingerprints of the trouble that's coming our way."

"We haven't had much time to practice," Jaradan said, keeping his eyes on her. "Learning to fly when you were expecting to work on walking can be a challenge."

"You think something's coming too?" she asked, looking up at him. "A feeling that we're going to be needed?"

"He said to tell you I need to be ready for a full deployment," Charley said, sitting down at the kitchen table across from Georgie, who was busy talking on a phone.

"He can't be serious, we just got you dressed," Gretta said, setting down a plate for her. "Best you eat something."

"She can wear her mother's suit," Georgie said, looking at Gretta as he ended his phone call. "It still needs to be taken in, it's a little long in the arms," looking back at Charley.

"She's right," he added, turning back to Gretta. "They're on call. We've lost contact with Ghost Team."

"What's that?" Charley asked, trying to eat her bacon and eggs while listening to the conversation. "I mean the ghost part."

"It's another ring bear, another team like you and your friend upstairs," Georgie said. "Its another girl, but they are a tracker team. It's from her cat, it's a Ghost Leopard."

"You mean she works with a real leopard, from the Himalayas," Charley asked, standing up at Gretta's urging as she finished her plate.

"My team doesn't hunt?" Charley asked, looking over to her.

"No, dear. Not exactly," Gretta replied, taking her apron off and laying over the chair. "They call on you when they want something dead. You find it, and then he kills it. You are a dangerous one to be around, you deal with death."

"Ghost was following a virus theft from some government lab. Anna thinks they found trouble, last location is a warehouse, somewhere in Ohio," Georgie said. "She's got the map and photos for the transfer. She holding out on the Feds, they're supposed to be coordinating this whole mess."

"Come with me," Gretta said, motioning her towards another doorway. "What we need is downstairs in the basement. If we have a team in trouble, we don't have much time before you get the call."

"Oh, nice. Feels comfortable down here," Charley remarked, looking around as they reached the basement.

"You're not bulletproof, so go with these two," Gretta said pointing to two dusky young teen girls that suddenly appeared from a dark corner of the room as they arrived in the basement. "I know, they have pointed ears. I'll explain later. They'll get you suited up."

"I'm Summer, and that's my sister, May," one of the girls said, leading her into a dressing room. "It's like a bodysuit," Summer explained as May picked up the clothing and held it up, "Battle armor. It goes under everything, and I mean *everything*."

"We're not elves, my Lady," May suddenly said, noting Charley's appraising glances at their ears as they helped her to get ready. "We're your team assistants."

"Gargoyle team," Summer said, a touch of pride in her tone, "The ones they call when it's serious."

"Or when things go sour." May added, showing a slight smile.

"Wear this over it," May said, helping Charley to don a deep cobalt blue one-piece suit. "It won't snag on anything, and absorbs the light. It absorbs your body heat, too."

"No laces," Charley said, snapping the fasteners over on the side of her boots. "That's a nice touch."

"This is your locator," Summer explained, holding up a small cell phone sized case before stuffing it into a pouch on the belt she had been holding on to. "I've added an extra for Sandi, just in case."

"The two longer pouches are your extra ammo, thirty rounds each. We'll grab your weapon on the way out," May said, helping to place the wide belt around Charley's waist, standing back to check their handiwork as it snapped together.

"A gun," Charley asked, her eyes widening at the thought, "I've never fired one in my life."

"Not a problem," May said, "It has a laser, just point and pull the trigger if you need to use it. Your mother wasn't one to hesitate in keeping some of those government boys ducking for cover when they got her upset. It has a silencer, so it's fun to shoot."

"I have to work with the government, too?" Charley asked, trying to keep up with the two girls.

"Not really, that's been rare lately," Summer said, "But they can be a real pain sometimes. Anna tolerates them cause they help pay the bills."

"It even has my name on it," Charley said, looking down at the gargoyle emblem on the side of the weapon as Summer handed it over to her.

"It slides into the holster in the middle of your back, on the belt," Summer said, handing her sister a band for Charley's hair. "When you're wearing your cloak, it can't be seen."

"We've been doing this for awhile," May added, seeing Charley's expression. "We're a little older than we look."

"Right," Charley said, looking from one to the other. "Listen, Georgie said I'm after a stolen virus. We have anything down here to deal with that? I mean, what happens if it gets loose."

"Oh, that's different," May said, frowning and giving her sister a look, "Can't shoot a bug."

"No... but you can burn them," Summer said slowly, a gleam coming to her dark eyes. "If you had a flamethrower."

"You can't be serious," May finally said, her eyes widening. "She hasn't been woken in over 500 years."

"Who? What?" Charley asked, looking from one to the other. "Can someone please explain?"

"Dragon team," Summer said, nodding her head a bit at the thought. "No bug ever made can withstand dragon fire. Roast them and toast them."

"There's a dragon team, too?" Charley asked, her own eyes widening at what the girls were saying.

"No, not anymore. No one can get to the ring," May said, giving a slight shrug with her shoulders.

"The tales say she swallowed it," Summer explained, seeing that Charley was about to ask. "So, she's been inactive for a while."

"Well, after 500 years, I'd say she's well rested," Charley let out. "Where do I find the ring bearer?"

"With the ring, he was wearing it at the time," May said quietly, "Which helps to explain why she's been sitting there idle."

"Oh," Charley sighed, "I see."

"How do we wake her up, I might not have much choice here.

"There's this vial, you pour it over her," May said, looking over to Summer, "but I'm not going to be the one getting caught with it. Gretta will have my hide placed on the office wall."

"You've been following all this?" Charley asked, looking upwards towards the attic as if she could see the gargoyle sitting there, watching with interest.

"Yes, the girls are correct." Jaradan replied. "We'll find the magic potion you need at the office, under the care of Granddon."

"We're both thinking of the dragon statue I saw in the office lobby, right?" Charley asked, checking the fit on her belt as she looked at the two. "The one that's about seven or eight feet tall."

"You two might want to look for any dragon symbols that might still be laying around, I'm going to go wake her up and see if she wants to enlist," Charley said. "I'm not waiting here for someone to give me some phone call."

"You ready?" she asked, noting the appearance of two heavy thick copper bands on his wrists as she appeared before him in the attic.

"This is not our usual fare, so don't get too caught up in all the excitement," he said, nodding and holding out a hand for Charley to grab.

"What's this?" Anna said, looking up in surprise as Jaradan lifted himself to his full height, standing behind Charley as they suddenly appeared in the middle of the office.

"I hear we have someone in trouble," Charley said, not waiting for more questions as Anna took in her appearance,

"We're on the job."

"I'll be needing the secret elixir, I'm taking what's left of the Dragon team with me," Charley let out, looking around the room for Granddon, "and the location."

"Hold on," Anna said, standing up as she recovered from their sudden arrival. "I just can't let you two loose on the world, it's not ready. *You're* not ready."

"So I've been advised," Charley replied, still looking for Granddon. "Granddon! Show your butt or I'll have an impatient gargoyle open your door and begin rearranging the furniture until we find that fairy dust," she let out loud enough to cause an echo. "Dragon team is moving out with us, so get your ass in gear."

"Wait, wait, wait… You can't take that dragon, she's on the standby list," Anna let out, her expression abruptly changing as she realized what was happening.

"Tell it to the boss," Jaradan said, leaving a deep lingering growl loose as he gave Anna a look. "The Lady is finding herself, step aside, or join in."

"We'll go get the dragon first," Anna said, picking up a folder from the desk, as a nervous Granddon appeared beside her, holding a dusty flask in his trembling hands.

"No one knows what her mood will be," Anna was saying as they appeared in the lobby. "She might still be upset."

"Let's find out," Charley muttered, walking over to the statue. "There's need, Dragon," pouring the deep blue liquid out on top of the dragon's head. "Time for action."

"This holds the map to your destination," Anna said, holding out the folder for Charley to take as they watched the deep color spread out, causing deep cracks to race across the shape.

Slowly, the dragon gave a slight movement, the motion

sending sections of the outer layers down to the floor, revealing the deep iridescent blue and green scales underneath.

"I had forgotten they're armor plated..." Charley said, amazed by the sight of the emerging creature. "Dragon scales. That'll come in handy."

"I was just getting comfortable," a new voice said, as the dragon's head turned to look at Charley. "I will tell you only once that I do not harken to the call of those who do not bear my ring."

"I see," Charley said, moving close to look in the dragon's eyes. "Then spit it up, or take a hike. Gargoyle team doesn't have time to waste," holding an open palm under the rows of teeth. "We're going into action, with or without you."

"You are very bold, for one who seems so young now," the voice replied, gauging the girl before her.

"Yeah, I'm just full of surprises, too. I'm finding myself," Charley said, placing one hand on her hip. "Choose."

"You bear his ring," the voice said, the eyes unwavering.

"I've got another hand, and lots of fingers left," Charley let out, along with a sigh. "Let's see how this works out."

"You agree, mighty one?" the dragon asked, her attention shifting over to Jaradan for a moment before returning to Charley.

"A team is not a pair, we are one as I have learned from the Lady," he replied, nodding his head.

"I like what I see... and hear," the dragon finally said, giving out a gurgle as a ruby ring appeared in Charley waiting hand. "As you say Lady, let's see where this takes us. I am *Ryuu*."

"Great," Charley let out, turning to a startled Granddon who nimbly caught the ring as she tossed it to him. "You've got five minutes to bring it back in my size. I've got to study this map before we go."

"It's not the sort of map you've seen before…" Anna started to say, before stopping as Charley raised one hand while looking down at the paper in the folder.

"Yeah, I've gathered that, give me a minute. I'm new to diagrams on spatial relationships," Charley muttered, frowning at what she was seeing.

"Does it say Ohio on it?" Jaradan asked, leaning over to peer at the paper. "Is there an X that marks the spot on it somewhere?"

"No, nosey. It says the earth is spinning on it's axis, while spinning around the sun, while we all spin through space, through the deepest part of some long lost universe," Charley let out, closing the folder and giving the gargoyle a fixed look, "and somewhere wrapped up in all this mess is the concept of time. Got it?"

"Granddon. Where's my ring?" she let out, looking around for him.

"Give him a break," Anna said in a quiet voice. "He had to take the elevator."

"You're beginning to have the same harried look my mom has," Charley said, raising an eyebrow as she glanced over to Anna.

Chapter Five

"There's certainly something going on in there," Charley said as they listened to the sound of gunfire echoing within the large structure. "Let's go find our girl."

"Over to the left," Jaradan advised, pointing towards the building. "She's on this side."

"Alright," Charley said, kneeling as they reached the hedges that grew around the parking lot. "Big guy, you stay near, but on the outside for now. We don't need them spotting us as soon as we make our entrance. Somebody might want to shoot me."

"*Ryuu* and I will enter at that far corner, that's close to where you say our team is pinned down. If they spot us, start taking out their vehicles. They can't run that far."

"Got it," Jaradan replied, looking around the lot for a metal lamppost. "I'll be atop that one, unless it starts to bend underneath me," pointing towards the end of the lot.

"To your right," *Ryuu* said, leading them towards a fallen row of shelves. "She's pinned down in there."

"Take it easy, it's just the rescue team," Charley whispered as they emerged from a portion of the shelving. "What's the big picture," looking over at the startled, blond haired girl lying on the floor.

"I think my leg's broke, and I'm caught up under this stuff," the girl replied, showing a weak smile at Charley's words. "I wasn't expecting anyone but the Feds when I discovered my locator got crushed."

"Where's your beast?" Charley asked, sliding closer to the girl. "I'm Charley by the way, Gargoyle team."

"This is *Ryuu*," Charley said, placing the second locator in Sandi's hand. "We'll get you out of here, I need to take care of that case, too."

"Sandi, Ghost team," Sandi said, giving a brief wave. "He's up there, on the metal rafters above the side wall."

"Okay, I see him," Charley whispered as she spotted the big cat. "Man, he's pretty," admiring soft gray color that slowly shading to white on his belly. "He seems to have his attention on something. What's his name?"

"*Fantôme*," Sandi replied, the pride showing in her voice. "The case, the vials. He's got his eyes on it, which means I have my eyes on it, too," trying not to let out a moan from her leg. "We almost had it when the deal between the two factions that met to negotiate the sell fell apart. Somebody noticed the case was missing after I snatched it, so they blamed each other, and then all hell broke loose. I got pinned when some explosives knocked the shelving over on me.

"One of them found the case, but he only made it a short distance before someone on the other side cut him down. That's why the case is over there now."

"Phantom, that fits him," Charley said. "I've never seen a Ghost Leopard before."

"*Ryuu*, if you would take over the watch on the case, we'll get this team out of here," Charley added, looking over to the dragon.

"That's a dragon, a real one. I thought you said gargoyle,"

Sandi said, watching in wonder as *Ryuu* left to begin her task.

"Yeah, it's a long story," Charley replied, showing a brief smile. "He's outside, keeping a eye out for unexpected company."

"Damn, they're still at it," Sandi let out as a bullet narrowly missed Charley, ricocheting off one of the metal frames.

"Don't move."

"Alright, we're going to have to do this the noisy way," Charley said, thinking on their options. "Jaradan, choose any of those fancy imports I saw out there and heave a couple through the wall from your side. We need a diversion so you can get in here to lift this metal off her."

"On it," the gargoyle replied. "The Feds have found us too, they're driving up the street with all their lights and sirens."

"*Ryuu*," Charley said, "The jig's up, this isn't just a rescue mission. Go ahead and guard the case in the open, kill anyone foolish to try and take away from you."

"Sandi, recall your team. Time to go, and we're all leaving together," Charley added, looking back at the prone girl, "I'll take care of the rest of this," the sound of automatic gunfire beginning from the other side of the warehouse, as a dark BMW came crashing through the ceiling, knocking over more shelves as it came in with a horrendous scream of rending metal and breaking glass.

"I think we've got their attention now," Sandi let out in the sudden silence that followed. "You guys know how to kick some ass."

"We're still new at it," Charley replied, moving around her to get a better view of the expanding battleground, "and we've got company to consider. The boys with the black Crown Vic's are here to reclaim their missing vials."

"The Feds," Sandi asked, shaking her head, "Figures they'd show, now it'll get dragged out."

"Holy crap," Sandi let out as another vehicle plowed through the wall, coming to rest against the far side.

"Hey, that was a VW," Charley let out, speaking to Jaradan. "Oh, wait... I get it... its a *bug*. Let's not get cute with the selection out there."

"I've got three running from this side," *Ryuu* reported. "The government team is engaged."

"All right, let me get her outside, I just got a wicked idea," Charley said, returning to Sandi. "Call kitty, I'm taking you out to the far side of the parking lot."

"You're slowing down," Charley said, looking up as Jaradan appeared beside them, placing both hands under the twisted metal frames.

"Couldn't find a door my size, had to make my own," he gasped, lifting up as Charley reached out to touch the leopard as he dropped down beside Sandi.

"You can let go now, I've got them outside," she said, reappearing beside the gargoyle. "Go watch over them, I think there's going to be a fire, big one."

"Good thing our team is mostly fireproof," Jaradan replied, dropping the heavy twisted metal with a screeching crash.

"Yeah," Charley said, listening to *Ryuu*. "They're got four in custody on the other side of the building, the government boys have two wounded. There's two others headed our way."

"If the evil ones escape us, they'll be free to continue their ways," Jaradan said, looking over to Charley.

"We're not finished here, be ready," Charley said, nodding her head in response to his look, "Gargoyle team doesn't take prisoners. I'm not feeling any remorse for terrorists. I know what they intended to do with the vials."

"You know the government intended the same thing then, why else develop it?" Jaradan said. "Its not right to let them get away with it, too."

"*Ryuu* and I were discussing that very thing," Charley replied, showing her brief smile again. "We've got that part covered. Anna is going to be a little upset."

"She'll learn to deal with it," Jaradan sighed, giving a wave as he left for the others outside.

"Hey, anyone else in here," a voice called out, as Charley began to walk towards the main entrance. "Come on out, we've got the place surrounded."

"Just me… and a few mythological creatures scattered about," Charley said, carefully emerging from the shelves as the government men came closer. "You might want to vacate the premises, guys. The gasoline from those cars might go at any time."

"Who are you?" the lead man asked, stopping the other with a raised hand. "You the cat woman?"

"No, she had to leave. I'm her replacement," Charley replied. "I don't have a nifty name or number. Creature girl sounds a bit pretentious, so just call me Charley. I suppose you could say I'm voice for my team."

"How about we just call you 'Kid' and haul your ass out of here," the other agent said, giving Charley a look over. "There isn't any gas leaking in here, you'd smell in a second."

"Watch it, Simmons," the first agent said, still studying Charley's appearance. "You know what we were told at the briefing. These folks come in, and they leave. We're not to interfere."

"They didn't say anything about her," Simmons muttered. "We've got men hurt, and maybe it's her fault. There isn't any cat woman with the case like we were told, and this one is just playing games."

"You want to play with me, Agent Simmons, like to play

with fire?" Charley asked, putting a hand on one hip as she gave him a look. "I've already warned you, time to go back to the office, boys."

"You won't be able to recover the vials," she added, looking back at the lead agent. "They were lost in the fire."

"This is bullshit, Rodgers, there isn't any fire," Simmons let out, coming up beside the other agent. "I say let's bring her in and get her name. We'll locate that case, it's got to be around here somewhere if she's still here. Those fuel tanks aren't leaking either, kid. They have to be punctured first, this isn't Hollywood."

"Duck, boys," Charley said, keeping her eyes on them as a car engine suddenly tore through the wall behind the pair, a spray of engine oil following as it cart wheeled across the floor and came to rest against a pallet of paint, the still spinning fan blades making a rapid metallic ding until they slowly came to a stop.

"What in hell did that?" Rodgers asked, spinning around to look at the torn hole in the metal wall.

"Gargoyle... a big one," Charley said, showing her smile again. "I needed a little more ventilation for the fire. Oh, and I'm guessing that would be an engine from one of your vehicles that just came sailing through here. The price you pay for parking close."

"That," Charley noted as a fuel tank came in through the gaping hole in the wall, landing nearby with a huge splay of gasoline across the floor, "is the fuel tank. Properly punctured," nodding at the leaking gashes on its side.

"It might not be from the same vehicle though," waving a hand across her nose at the spreading fumes from the gas as it spread out across the floor. "I asked him to toss the one with the most in it."

"It's best that you guys grab your friends and head for the street. Leave the rest to me, the little red haired girl," Charley advised, smiling again as *Ryuu* could be seen peering around one end of the shelves. "I've been told by an expert that there's going to be one hell of a fire in here."

"That's a real fire breathing dragon, and she isn't from Hollywood either," Charley said, seeing the shock on their faces. "I'll give you three minutes to run, after that you only have yourselves to blame if you lose anyone else, or she singes your backsides."

"Run, boys, run!" Charley yelled out as *Ryuu* reared up and let loose with an ear splitting roar that echoed across the warehouse. "She can't tell time."

"Impressive, I like the way you guys work," Sandi let out as they all watched the inferno go up, a huge mushroom shaped ball of fire raising some 200 feet into the air as the gas fumes and paint caught.

"I'm going to like some aspects of this job," Charley said, leaning back against Jaradan as the flames reflected on her face, "and they pay me, too."

"What happened to the case?" Sandi asked, grimacing as Jaradan lifted her up in his arms.

"Oh, that thing. I left it with the four who got caught... after I asked them if they still wanted it," Charley said, her eyes still on the blaze. "The Feds will find some of their bones once that place cools down. I'm sure they're looking for them since they disappeared as soon as they had their backs turned. That part doesn't look good in the report."

"Okay, gang. Mission accomplished. Come on *Ryuu*," smiling at the dragon as she appeared next to them. "Let's go home."

"May, Summer," Charley called out, as they appeared in

the basement. "We've got somebody hurt here. We need the witch doctor, or whoever we use for times like this."

"I'll take over on this," Gretta said, coming down the stairs behind them. "You might want to let Anna know how things went, besides what's being shown on the news," giving the dragon a glance. "I imagine she's biting her nails by now."

"I wasn't expecting to see you here. How's my cousin doing?" she asked, keeping her eyes on *Ryuu*.

"Still giving me indigestion," *Ryuu* replied, sitting back on her haunches and folding her wings back. "He needs more time."

"Figures," Gretta said, nodding her head slightly at the comment. "He always gave me indigestion too."

"I'll wait here," *Ryuu* said, looking over to Charley. "One of these fine looking girls can give me and the kitty the grand tour while you're consoling Anna."

"Prisoners, Anna? What was I supposed to do with prisoners?" Charley asked, with hands on hips as she looked at Anna. "I watch the news, one of them shows up on prime time with a busted lip, and I get charged with violating their rights. The system has become so distorted that if you kill them in a battle, you're the hero. Slap them for trying to destroy the lives of thousands of people and you're facing two to four in the local dungeon, with no visitation rights."

"My team has opted for killing them, that's what we do," she ended with. "I'm not going to do this job halfway, and we've all decided we're not going to be called back to do the job a second time."

"If it makes you feel any better, I gave those guys a choice, it being my first mission. I double-checked their motivation by asking if they still wanted those vials."

"I see," Anna sighed, leaning forward in her chair, keeping her eyes on Charley. "I'm beginning to think you're more than we bargained for."

"Careful, that'd mean I earn a higher pay rate," Charley remarked, unsnapping the front of her clothing. "Mission accomplished, no team members left behind. Gargoyle team is offline until the world calls on us again."

"Your next mission briefing is here at 10," Anna said, sitting back in her chair. "The cries of the innocent won't allow a longer delay now that you've been tested by your first mission."

"This is the type you're best at, finding evil and removing it before other innocent lives are affected and destroyed. You're going to church, dress appropriately."

"You earned yourself a bonus for coming to the aid on another team, which shows initiative, and for completing the mission. Don't go spending it all in one place."

"I don't know how you were able to figure out the map so quickly, and I don't think I want to. You might want to give some consideration to another name if you're taking on a third partner, something that tells me if I'm biting my nails over the two of you or all three."

"I'll give it some thought," Charley said, raising an eyebrow at the idea. "I've got dance practice this evening," suddenly remembering and giving the gargoyle a quick glance, "How about we go swimming after that. I know this spot that's popular with some of the local boys."

"I could use a nice bath," Jaradan replied. "I'm covered with soot," returning her grin, "I can't wait to see you on the diving board."

"I've noticed you have this deep, unwavering fascination with the human female form," Charley said, shaking her head at him as she reached out to take his hand. "Let's go home, mister. Maybe we should discuss where this comes from, I'm a good listener. If I had any friends, you could ask them."

"Give my bonus to Sandi, I don't need any extra," she added, turning to look at Anna as they both vanished.

"Nice architecture, it even has cute little concrete gargoyles sitting on each of the eaves," Charley finally said. "A little weather worn, but you can tell what they are," looking over the photo of the church again. "I guess we're going to see the inside for ourselves."

"Yes," Anna said, tapping the open folder on her desk with her pen. "This one has been a pressing issue, one that's been growing worse. I hate holding the ones that involve children."

"We're on it," Charley sighed, reaching down and picking up the folder. "According to this report, it's better to wait until everyone else leaves the place, so we'll plan on doing that. Gargoyle team will go in tonight."

"Great," Anna said, looking a little relieved. "This is one I've been waiting to clear off the list. Those who prey on children are nothing more than twisted monsters in my book."

"In that case, we'll make him an example. He won't simply vanish, to be replaced by another of like mind," Charley said, looking over at Anna. "I'm with you on this one."

"You alright?" Charley asked, noting the gargoyle's set expression.

"I can sense the wail of those affected, the sound lingers in my mind," Jaradan replied. "This place is to the east of us which makes the time different. I feel we should arrive an hour before dusk, the last of the parishioners should have left by then."

"Sounds like a plan," Charley said, nodding at the

suggestion. "I don't think we'll be needing *Ryuu* on this one. I hadn't planned on burning the place to the ground, although there are some who would applauded the thought if the truth was known to all."

"I'll deal with the one we want," Jaradan said, his tone reflecting his emotions. "It has been far too long since his kind was left a warning."

"I'm taking my cloak on this one," Charley said, spreading it out around her shoulders and raising the hood up over her hair to obscure her face. "How do I look?"

"Like one of the Shadow Demons from the third ring of Hades," Jaradan replied. "Nice, I like it."

"Only you would say something so sweet," Charley replied, picking up the folder and studying the map for a moment. "Let's go."

"I see you're bringing your pouch," he let out, reaching out to take her hand.

"Can you get in that way?" Charley asked as they stood in the shadows of an adjacent building, gazing upwards at the bell tower high above them.

"Oh, ye of little faith," Jaradan sighed, looking back down at her. "This is not my first time entering a church."

"Oh, I guess not. I suppose we should be grateful that it's not all bricked up, with a loudspeaker shoved in it," Charley said, returning his look. "We had best pick up the pace. There's a child in need somewhere in there."

Walking up to the large doors that faced he main street, Charley grasped the handle of one and gave a strong pull, opening the heavy door enough for her to squeeze through, "Shame there weren't any photos of the inside," she muttered, looking around the room she found herself in as the door swung closed behind her.

Passing a large granite font that occupied one corner, Charley quietly made her way through another doorway, allowing her mind to lead her along the rows of pews until she reached the ones that were closest to the altar, the space dimly light by several candles that had been set upon it.

Seeing the movement in the low light, she leaned against the railing that separated the pews from the altar, watching for a moment.

"Don't you just hate it when those little zipper's get stuck, and just refuse to budge?" Charley asked, breaking the silence as she faced the faint figures. "His mom probably sewed it closed, knowing where he'd be this evening."

"What?" Is someone there?" a male voice asked, the tone displaying his shock at being discovered.

"Just me, padre," Charley replied as the man's face appeared beside the candles, using the light to look around the area. "The red haired girl."

"It's Father, Father Angelino," the priest replied, quickly lighting additional candles to provide more light. "Who are you?"

"Just a passer by. I thought I heard the cry of a child, and came to help," Charley replied, keeping her attention on the man as the sound of scampering feet could be heard running down a rear area from the altar.

"Ah, yes. As you've said, the lad was in a dilemma, the zipper stuck as to prevent him from using the facilities properly. One of my altar boys, he sought my assistance. We were just finishing up the business of the church in here, my child," he added, peering closely at Charley's draped figure. "The church is now closed for the evening. It would be best that you return in the light of day."

"How did you get in, are you alone?" he asked, lighting another candle, his hand beginning to shake as he held the match to the wick.

"Alone, Tony, but for the one above us both," Charley said quietly, giving a slight motion upwards with her eyes before returning her gaze to the priest, "The one who knows all."

"It's Angelino, Father Angelino, as I've said," the priest said, glancing around into the shadows that surrounded them. "Is there someone else here?"

"Ah, sorry," Charley said, pulling the hood back away from her face. "I thought you were Anthony O'Brien, from the south side of Chicago. I was raised thinking we're never alone, but tell me Tony, what kind of *father* wants to do those kind of things to children?"

"You should go, now," Angelino said, his voice taking on a more authoritive tone as he realized he faced only a young girl. "The church is closed, and you must depart."

"Closed," Charley repeated with a sigh. "I thought this was the house of your God. Isn't he always in residence, listening to the pleas and prayers of those in need? Must I now wait outside on the street, listening to the cries of those who have been damned by you, until the light of day falls once more upon your doors and all are welcomed in?

"Was it something I said... *Tony*? I thought us girls were safe in a church like this."

"Go now, before I summon the police," Angelino let out suddenly, his face changing expression as he glanced around again. "You are not welcome here. Go!"

"Why, Tony? Do you need the time to find that boy that ran past? I can tell you exactly where he's huddled. I can hear his tears as they silently fall upon the floor of the room he has hidden himself in, still shaking from his fear. Ever so grateful that his own prayers have finally been answered."

"Don't worry, I'm leaving," Charley said, replacing her hood around her face. "I had wanted to see the face of evil before me, I was told it would help me deal with what would follow. You've earned your fate, I am certain of that, and I am not sorry to see you go. Perhaps it will bring some closure to those you've hurt when it becomes known."

"Oh, I brought an old friend of the church along with me," Charley said, taking a hand and pointing up towards the dark rafters above them. "You might have heard of him, his name is *Nex*."

"Didn't they teach you in church school that we reap what we sow?" Charley quietly asked, watching the priest's face go pale in the candlelight as he slowly looked upwards.

"Did you hear?" Darlene asked, looking over with a shocked expression as Charley entered the living room. "They found his heart laying on the altar."

"Whose heart, mom?" Charley asked, sitting down on the sofa next to her as she glanced at the news program.

"Some priest's, it's all over the news," William said entering from the kitchen with a plate of chicken strips in his hand. "They say his entire chest was ripped open from the throat down, and then the heart torn out as if by a wild beast. They say the place is covered in his blood."

"Gruesome, I hadn't heard anything on that," Charley replied, giving him a glance. "Who did it?"

"A gang, they think," Darlene said, her attention still on the news. "There was this eight hundred pound granite font, for the blessing water you know, that was knocked over as well. They used the water to rinse off, and tipped it over so the water ran across the floor and underneath the doors. That's what led to the discovery."

"They think it might be three of four people involved at least. They even climbed up and tore off one of the concrete statues from the roof. They found it on the altar, surrounded by all that blood."

"What's your plans for the day," William asked, looking over to Charley. "More work?"

"Oh, no I've earned a break, so I'm catching up on my washing, doing the linens and stuff," Charley said. "I have an *Otea* coming up and I need to spend some time working on my attire. I need to go buy the materials for more tassels, and have to relearn how to make a skirt, my old one is beginning to fall apart on me."

"Interesting touch," Anna said, glancing up at Charley as she entered the office. "I never would have thought of weighing his heart against one of Ma'at's white feathers, then leaving his heart on the floor where it got tossed."

"I brought the scales of Osiris with me, I wanted to make sure," Charley replied. "When other ancient Gods agreed, I knew I was justified. Didn't want to toss and turn all night, thinking I had made a mistake, and I especially didn't want to end up like Georgie. Fearful to stand so close to him again."

"I guess you got a good look at the reports, that stuff wasn't mentioned in the news. My mom would have told me. I got an ear full on all the other details, although they differ on where the heart was found."

"Well, that's one your mother never would have thought of. As I understand it, she was more blunt in her approach," Anna said. "Don't tell me where you got a feather of truth, I don't want to know."

"You wouldn't believe me anyway," Charley said, looking around the office. "The place is buzzing, is there another operation going on."

"Well, Sandi just left, still using her crutches. Her bone was fractured, but she's all patched up, and healing just fine. Still gushing over you, can't say enough nice things to anyone who will listen," Anna said, smiling at the memory. "Have you got a new name for me yet?"

"Oh, that," Charley replied, watching as two child sized boys passed by, each giving her a bow. "I'm still working on it."

"This place feels like someone just stole Pandora's vase," Charley noted. "Is there something for my team?"

"No, you're off, remember? Wolf team is on cattle mutilations, and Eagle is helping with a search job out west, no real evil there. Mostly avarice for the others today," Anna replied, waving her towards the door. "So off with you."

"You think she believed you?" Granddon asked, peering around from the back of Anna's chair as Charley headed off to do some shopping.

"Let's hope so," Anna replied, opening the folder she had closed when Charley came in. "I should start calling them the hit squad."

"Perhaps the Shadows of Death," Granddon suggested quietly, slowly looking back up at Anna.

"Where we going this time?" Charley asked, taking the offered hand in her own, her eyes on Jaradan's.

"Something I wanted to show you. You had asked me about dimensional jumps, something you said Georgie mentioned," he replied, allowing a mental image to fill his mind. "Just use this, same as when we went to Egypt for those scales."

"We're here," she said quietly, looking around at the dusty red scene before them, "Looks like the place is abandoned, and it happened a long, long time ago."

"Yes, they left many years ago," he replied, watching her as Charley turned to look at where she had brought them. "They will begin to come back now, they will know you have returned. The life will soon follow."

"A great battle was once fought here," he added, watching as the winds carried some of the red dust down the empty street they stood on. "Evil once tried to rule over good here, in one of it's many disguises. Your mother faced it alone, something she said she had to do."

"This place looks like it's in sad shape," Charley said, still looking around at the stone structures, before glancing up at the sky above them. "Spooky."

"Who changed the sky?" she asked, giving it another look before turning towards Jaradan, "Or did it always look that way?"

"No, it once shone bright, and filled with billowing clouds," he said, following her gaze for a moment before looking at her. "The rains brought the crops, the river ran full of fish and other creatures lived the land. What you see is a result of what can happen when we face evil. There can be a price that must be paid."

"The people were saved," he said, anticipating her next question, "Moved elsewhere. She needed the energy of the planet itself to overcome that which slinked and crawled the land," his eyes still on her.

"She was prepared to destroy the planet itself, if that was what it took. She had the ability."

"She could destroy entire worlds." Charley said, looking up at him before looking around them once more.

"It is said by some that the only difference between Angels and Demons is their purpose," he said quietly, meeting her eyes when Charley finally turned back to look at him.

"Come, there is an ancient temple near here, up at the high castle. I thought you might be interested in seeing it."

"There's someone using our swimming hole," Charley whispered, looking through the glass into the pool area where splashing and yells could be heard. "I'd like to rinse this dust off me."

"Their clothing is over there on the far edge," Jaradan noted, joining her as best he could at the office window by leaning over, "and the lights are off."

"It'd be a real shame if they mysteriously vanished," Charley mused, giving the gargoyle a quick glance before peering back out at the pool again, "the clothes, I mean… a real shame."

"It'd be damn strange if the clothing were to be found in the lockers in the girl's changing room later," he replied, standing back up, "Just imagine the shock and dismay."

"Hey, where did you put my towel?" Walsh asked, rubbing at his eyes. "They must have put too much chlorine in here this time, my eyes are burning."

"I think I left everything over next to the door," Peter, another boy, replied while climbing up the ladder. "I'll grab it if you can't handle some water in your eyes."

"I have problems with the chemicals they use in pools," Walsh, replied, giving the boy a dark look that went unnoticed in the dim light. "That's why my dad never had one put in at our house."

"I thought it had something to do with city codes, and the taxes they tack on," Jeffery said from edge of the pool. "That's what my dad was saying awhile back."

"Just grab it, okay?" Walsh let out. "If you two hadn't tossed that stuff in here last time, maybe they wouldn't have put so much in."

"Save it," Jeffery replied. "It was your idea as I recall."

"It's not over here," Pete yelled back, looking around. "Hey, all our clothes are missing too!"

"Something's in here with us," Walsh suddenly said, listening as a deep rumbling growl seemed to come from the far dark end of the pool, the sound rising in intensity before falling off.

"Oh, damn. There's it is," Peter yelled, spotting a large dark shadow as it moved closer to the water. "It's getting closer. Let's get out of here."

"Yeah, let's split," Jeffery cried out as a huge splash was heard, "Something's in the pool."

"We can't yet, my clothes," Peter yelled back, backing up to the doors. "All our stuff is gone."

"Screw this," Walsh suddenly yelled, his fear showing in his voice as he kicked out with his legs while he heaved himself up on the pool's edge. "Ahh. Something just tried to grab my leg, it's under the water."

"Run," Jeffery screamed as Jaradan lifted himself up from the water with an ear splitting roar that echoed around the room, his claws extended as he held his arm out while lifting his wings over his head.

"What the hell is going on," Walsh yelled as the fire alarm went off, almost falling on the wet floor as he tried to reach the doors ahead of Jeffery, the sounds of the emergency bells merging with their own cries as they fought each other to get the doors open.

"Oh," Charley gasped, reaching out to lean against a wall

for balance as the laughter overtook her, holding her stomach with one hand. "I'm going to wet myself, that was the funniest thing I've seen in years."

"Well, some parts were." Jaradan agreed, hauling himself out of the water.

"Yeah," Charley giggled, before sliding down the wall to the floor while laughter overtook her once more. "*Some parts* were."

"You better hurry up," Jaradan suggested, shaking the water off himself, "I hear the sirens. We should go somewhere to eat while they're discovering naked boys lingering in the local area. Someplace that has pie, blueberry is preferred."

"Okay," Charley sighed, finally recovering and standing back up, "Let's come back in a few hours. I should take a quick shower when we get back before we enjoy the pool, it's best to leave it cleaner than when we found it."

"Tell me," Charley said quietly from her position, sitting on the end of the diving board where she could look down. "How come no one has mentioned what happened to my mother. I mean, how I ended up getting adopted."

"She wanted it that way," Jaradan sighed, stretching out and resting his head up against the shallow edge of the pool. "She wanted you to be older."

"Older than what, an elephant?" Charley asked, giving out a rude noise. "How does everyone know what she wanted?"

"The will," the gargoyle replied, still trying to get himself to float. "Everything's written down in the will. I'm not to speak of them... until you're older."

"Why not, you under a curse of something?" Charley asked, leaning back on her hands as she peered down at him.

"It's in the will," he repeated. "I can't seem to learn this trick you showed me, I keep sinking."

"You can turn to stone, that might have something to do with it." Charley pointed out, giving him a slight smile.

"Can you tell me who the boss of the company is?" Charley asked, carefully standing back up on the board.

"No, you'll discover that on your own." Jaradan said, giving out a moan of disgust as he found the bottom once more.

"Oh wait, don't tell me…" Charley said, making her own noise of disgust. "That's in the will, too."

"Am I really named after a spider?"

"You're discovering that your entire existence is a mystery, and don't you look nice all naked," Jaradan replied, changing the subject as he looked back up at her, standing up to catch her as she lifted up both arms and let herself fall forward. "My own past isn't much different, I've learned to deal with it."

"Did you tell Anna that you've learned to travel using the images from books and mental images yet?" catching her easily.

"No, I was getting the impression that she thinks I talk too much," Charley replied, heading over to the edge of the pool. "Try it again, only this time spread out your wings first, they'll keep you buoyant."

"Now, where did I leave my towel," glancing around the pool area, before looking back at him with a raised eyebrow.

Chapter Six

"A stock broker?" Charley asked, lowering the folder enough to see over the top of it at Anna with a questioning look. "I thought they usually did themselves in, just after getting their quarterly reports."

"Not this one," Anna said. "He's more interested in depriving others of their life's savings, and causing them to end it all."

"Sucks them dry and tosses them aside," Charley mused, glancing back over the folder's report. "Up in the big bad city, I should be careful."

"He has own suite, with a wide open balcony on the twentieth floor that he uses to sit and look out over his domain, when he's not hosting wild lavish parties on it," Anna said, giving out a little snort of disgust. "Go get him."

"Well, according to this, he's hosting tonight. What a coincidence," Charley said, looking back at Anna. "I haven't gone to a *adult* fling before, I might want to stay for awhile… to watch."

"You might want to dress up a bit," Anna said, noting the jeans. "Stop in around 10 tonight, I'll have something proper for the event, and Summer's a fine makeup artist. Don't drink whatever they're serving, they're prone to putting something in young girl's drinks."

"I put a photo in there, should make it easy."

"Gottcha," Charley replied, looking over to Jaradan. "When's the last time you did a high rise?"

"Always liked them myself, there's usually a nice breeze at the top," he replied, looking around the office before bringing his gaze to Anna. "Anything else we need to know?"

"That's it for now," Anna said, beginning to look uncomfortable under his stare. "Let me know how it goes."

"Sure, I always do." Charley replied, reaching out for the gargoyle's hand. "See you later then."

"Ever notice that Anna gets this little quiver to her lip when she's under stress?" Charley asked, looking over to Jaradan as the attic appeared around them.

"Interesting, now what would make her feel uncertain or nervous," Jaradan said quietly settling down on the floor.

"Well, I might have part of the answer," Charley said, her attention back on the open folder in her hand. "The office staff is too efficient, this top page is marked 1 of 4."

"So?" Jaradan asked.

"So, there's only three pages here, including the photo," Charley replied, giving him a look. "*Comprende?*"

"Ah, I do indeed," the gargoyle said. "We're playing super spy after all."

"So it would seem," Charley said quietly, closing the folder and tapping it against one leg as she thought. "We better be careful on this one. Something's up."

"Maybe the broker is not the mission," Jaradan mused, giving her a glance. "Maybe *Ryuu* should come along as well, she can stand guard on a parapet."

"Yeah, I'm getting a weird feeling on this one," Charley

sighed, tossing the folder down on the table beside her. "I'm heading off to get us some lunch. You want fried chicken brought back?"

"I want to get this water out of my ears," he replied, tapping one side of his head. "Georgie told me to go stick my head in the oven."

"It wouldn't fit. Try standing on your head," Charley advised. "I'm asking Summer and May on something nice to wear to the event. I'm sure they'd know what I need."

"Since it'll be after sunset, maybe you should bring them along. If something's got Anna spooked, they might prove helpful," Jaradan muttered, trying to stick a finger down one ear. "It's probably those numbnutty Feds again."

"Hmm, the girls..." Charley said, slowly nodding her head, "they're part of the team, too."

"You wearing a dress tonight?" he asked, giving up on his ear.

"No... I think a light revealing top with long flowing sleeves, maybe along with a nice wrap around skirt in Earth tones. With some shoes that match the outfit, of course. After all, I'm supposed to be this fashion model."

"What's sunset got to do with anything?" Charley asked, placing a hand on one hip as she gave him her inquiring look.

"What time we leaving?" Summer asked, excited at the prospect of going out with the team.

"10, the time Anna wanted me cooling my heels over at the office," Charley replied, checking her own appearance in the mirror. "Nice, I love what you've done with my hair. I'll stand out like the Princess at the Ball."

"Actually, all three of us are going to share the limelight tonight, I think," Charley added, giving the two girls an appraising glance. "Perhaps we shouldn't be too hasty in tossing anyone out into the street, maybe we can enjoy the evening out before mixing business with pleasure."

"Yes," May replied, smiling at the idea. "It's been years since we went out anywhere like this."

"You know, you two have this Victorian era look about you in those gowns," Charley noted, giving them another lingering look. "Don't ever tell how old you two are, I don't want to know."

"Impressive," Jaradan sighed, giving Charley's new top a lingering look. "I just love the swell of your breasts that are showing."

"It's called cleavage," Charley replied, giving herself a glance downward, "Let's hope I don't show more than this."

"Why not?" Jaradan asked, giving out a slight laugh. "Wearing that, it's clear to all that you have plenty to show."

"Oh, hush. You'll make me blush," Charley said. "Summer picked it out for me. I like it."

"I picked out the skirt," May remarked as the two girls joined them, "you can't tell she's got her weapon under there."

"No," Jaradan said, giving Charley's skirt another look. "Can I see where?"

"No, you can't see where, mister, and no trying to peek. Remember who you are," Charley sighed, shaking her head before looking over to *Ryuu*. "Are we ready?"

"Let me know if he gets out of hand," *Ryuu* said, nodding towards the gargoyle. "I can toast his backside from twenty feet away."

"Yes, we're ready to move out," the dragon added, exchanging looks with Jaradan.

"Must be nice to have money, especially other people's

money," Charley said quietly as they looked down at the party going on below them.

"He's shameless, and has lousy taste in some of his friends." May noted, poking her sister and pointing at one of the women.

"That one looks out of place." Summer said, holding in a giggle with one hand. "She's dressed for the street corner."

"Must be a special guest," Charley said, following the object of their attention. "I like the way that other girl is dressed, the one by the railing."

"Sweet," May said, nodding her head in unison with her sister. "She looks like she can hold an intelligent conversation, we should find out. Have to crash in somewhere."

"Hey, I'm Charley," Charley said, walking up beside the quiet girl where she still leaned against the edge.

"Oh, hey back, I'm Amber," the girl replied, coming out of her reverie at the sound of Charley's voice. "Nice outfit, is that from around here somewhere?" she asked, taking in Charley's clothing.

"No, it was commissioned just for me," Charley said. "For this evening's get together. Are you in the fashion field?"

"No, my mother," Amber said, turning and placing her back against the rail. "She brought me here to let everyone who's anyone see my face. She thinks the best guys will show up."

"Have they?" Charley asked, joining her in looking at the groups inside through the glass doorway of the suite.

"I haven't seen one yet, just the usual crowd you see wherever you go," Amber said, lifting one hand to point. "That's Harold, our gracious host. He's been busy, trying to discover someone who's not wearing anything under their dress. He'll find one sooner or later."

"I heard that he found out that a *she* was a *he* last year.

Mother told me he had to seek therapy."

"He seems to have made a full recovery," May came out with, watching as the man patted one of the girls passing by on the backside.

"I'm told he has nude photos plastered all over his den… of his conquests," Amber added, seeing Charley's questioning look. "My mother, no doubt, got plastered there more than once."

"Oh, hold onto something girls," Amber suddenly let out, nodding towards the hall. "Some real looking guys just came in."

"That's my cue, see ya's," she said quietly moving towards the doors.

"Well, well, small world," Charley said, letting the two sitting up above them know, "It's those two Agents from the fire, the ones so disappointed that they arrived too late to recover those vials."

"They're late again," Summer said, glancing down at her watch. "It's after ten, the game is in play."

"I'll get close to them, just like one of the other admirers they'll attract," May said, wandering after Amber.

"Yeah, everybody keep alert, we don't know what's really going on here," Charley said. "Harold is the target for us… but I'm getting a feeling that he has his own list in mind, and maybe he's on someone else's list, too."

"There's something strange about him, I'm getting the feeling that I've seen him before somewhere."

"There's a weird feeling in there." May said, glancing around the area as she hurried back out to Summer and Charley after a few minutes, "Makes me feel uncomfortable, and itchy all over."

"So, he's into something strange," Charley mused, "I'm

going to wander around in there myself, be ready to grab him if he gets out of hand."

"Maybe he's expecting us," Jaradan mused from his perch above her. "My intuition says something's very odd is going on here."

"Maybe he's expecting trouble, I'm getting a feeling that he's veiled himself with something," Charley replied. "Something different from what the girls are feeling when they get close."

Keeping to the side, Charley maneuvered herself around the room, keeping a look out for the two agents who seemed to have vanished into one of the other rooms.

"Where's the new guys," Charley asked, seeing Amber sitting alone on the sofa, looking distressed.

"Oh, that Harold just came by and grabbed them with each arm. Took them back that way, probably went into his den," Amber said, giving a hallway a look of disgust, "I guess he's isn't so *cured* after all."

"That's too bad, I feel for you," Charley said, giving her a glance before looking down the hallway. "That way?"

"Yeah, you can't miss it. There are these odd carvings all around the door," Amber said, grabbing another drink from a tray as servant brought it past her. "Looks like hieroglyphics or something."

"Hey, did you see that?" Amber asked as Charley moved past her, stopping to peer down the hall.

"What?" Charley replied, looking around the room to see what Amber had remarked on.

"That piece of colored glass up there," Amber said, now using her glass for a pointer as she leaned back against the sofa. "It just glowed when you went past."

"A crystal, like the others in the attic," Charley said quietly, seeing the glow again as she passed on by. "This is getting interesting."

Coming to the door marked by wide wooden frames around the sides and top, she came to a stop, listening at the door for any sounds.

"That's not nice," a voice behind her suddenly said, causing Charley to whirl around, "Perhaps you had better come with me," the man said, giving Charley a dour look.

"No, I like it here just fine," Charley finally said, taking in the servant's muscular appearance. "I've decided to stay."

"You can't go in there, Aileana," he said, quickly reaching out to grab her by an arm, his hand like a steel vise, "even if you wanted to. He doesn't want you, or your kind here. He pays me to watch the doorway, and to get rid of the ones like you. The ones who come snooping where they have no business."

"Like my ring?" Charley asked, seeing the man's face go pale as he noticed it on her hand, "Looks like it reminds you of something."

"It matters not, the master will deal with that one," the man snarled, recovering his composure as he tightened his grip even more. "Besides, the creature can't get past the portal either."

"He won't need to," Charley said, letting a slight smile show as May grabbed the man by the back of his neck. "Thanks for touching me, it helps to know what's on the other side of the door."

"Go set him on a seat somewhere, spill a drink on him and leave the glass in his hand," Charley said, looking over to Summer as the lifeless body fell down in a loose heap.

"Will do, boss," May said, grabbing one of his arms to drag him with, "There's something strange about that door, I can feel it."

"Yeah, me too," Charley said, taking a step back to take another look at the symbols carved into the door's frame. "You guys seeing what I'm seeing," she asked trying to send a mental image to the two on the roof.

"Strange indeed," Jaradan mused, as Charley suddenly appeared beside them, using one hand to keep the wind from blowing her hair around her face.

"It's a protected doorway. One that goes nowhere," he said, slowing nodding his head at his conclusion.

"It's a trap," *Ryuu* added. "A clever one, too."

"Can you explain a little more," Charley asked, looking from one to the other. "I'll need to get in there, if that's where he's hiding."

"It's a trap specially made for one of your abilities," *Ryuu* said, moving closer. "You can't just reappear on the other side, it isn't there. If you recall, he said it was a portal."

"But I saw his memories of the room," Charley said. "He's seen the inside. It's real, it exists."

"Yes, but stop to think on it," Jaradan said, looking down at her. "He's seen it when the door was open, and he called you by your mother's name."

"That's shows he knew you could just show up on the other side of the door. He wanted you to try it," *Ryuu* added. "He made it a challenge for you."

"He works for someone else, so maybe that's the one who wanted me to try it. The servant was just the messenger, a disposable asset," Charley said. "That a pretty evil thing to do."

"Now we're getting somewhere," Jaradan said, looking at *Ryuu* before turning back to Charley. "We know the one we're after is hiding behind some kind of magick."

"A magick that's intended to warn him of you, and he's laid

out a trap, as if he was expecting you to show up one day," *Ryuu* said.

"Not one intended to capture you, either," Jaradan added.

"Someone wants you out of the picture for good."

"It's someone who knows of my mother too... Hey, maybe he's scared of me," Charley said, giving them both a quick look, "but I still need to get into the room."

"Think on it," Jaradan finally said, giving her a look, "What would Aileana do?"

"Who wouldn't fear death," *Ryuu* mused, giving Jaradan a glance as Charley vanished.

"Hello, anybody in there?" Charley let out as she pounded on the door again.

"Oh, Agent Simmons, its you in here. I thought this was the girl's bathroom," Charley said, greeting him with a wave as the door was opened from the inside. "I didn't realize you guys did parties, too."

"Hey there, Agent Rodgers," she added while stepping in, seeing him standing in another room. "Still looking for those vials?"

"Well, small world," Rodgers let out, giving Charley an appraising look as he stepped back to see her better. "I think you've found the wrong room this time."

"You had better run along home, girly," Simmons remarked, eyeing her top, "Before your mother finds out what you're wearing, or not wearing."

"Oh, I think my mother would approve," Charley said, stepping further into the room. "I hope you guys didn't get singed last time we met."

"Look here, creature girl, or whoever you are today," Simmons said, lifting a hand and motioning back towards the door with his thumb, "The exit is that way. Last time we stopped to have a chat, we both got reamed by our boss in the big office."

"He didn't believe the part about the dragon, huh?" Charley asked, peering around the room. "I guess you had to be there. You guys should carry a camera."

"Who's come knocking, Mr. Simmons?" another voice asked, his form hidden by the doorframe of the room Rodgers was standing in. "Someone we know?"

"It's just some crazy kid, Mr. Jones," Simmons said, turning to face the doorway as he replied to the question. "We've met her before. I'm trying to get rid of her," his voice fading out as he turned to look back at Charley and his eyes met *Ryuu*'s, the slight wisps of smoke coming her nostrils causing him to take a step back.

"Sssh," Charley whispered, holding a finger to her lips as she faced Simmons, "Let's pretend fire breathing dragons really do exist, and if you get one upset… well, you know what happens after that. It's all in your last report."

"It'd be best if you just stood still, and very, very quiet," Charley said, giving the agent a pat on one shoulder as she moved past him towards the other room. "She bites, too."

"Didn't mean to barge in like this, I was exploring this place you have here, Harold," Charley let out as she rounded the corner, seeing the one she was interested in sitting behind a large wooden desk.

"We know each other don't we, child," Harold said, sitting back in his chair as he took in Charley's appearance, his eyes staying on hers as Charley moved closer.

"You've met her, too?" Rodgers asked, a slight tone of surprise in his voice, looking back at the man behind the desk.

"Oh, not in person… but in a manner of speaking," Harold

replied, beginning to show some discomfort at Charley's presence.

"One hears tales of the bogey man, those things that go bump in the night," he slowly said, turning to attention to the agent for a moment before looking back at the girl before him. "It's like that. You know what it is when you see it."

"Couldn't have said it better myself," Charley said, nodding her head. "Sorry to interrupt, I hope your business with the government is finished," giving a small dark crystal sitting on the desk a quick curious glance.

"Giving advice to the current political system?" she asked, giving Rodger a look. "Using magick... isn't that cheating?"

"Why no, its a long standing practice," Harold sighed. "Most governments of recent times have employed my services at one time or another. The British are even known to have used astrologers and such during the last world war."

"Yeah, so I've heard," Charley replied. "I can guess which side of that war you were on, Harold. I think your team lost that one."

"And what team are *you* on today?" Harold asked, tapping his fingers on the arm of his chair as his eyes fell on her rings.

"Oh, I'm with the First team, the first one they call on to deal with the likes of you, Harold," Charley replied, placing one hand on a hip. "I brought them all with me this time. Want to meet them?"

"I'm afraid that won't be happening today, you're the last of them to come calling," he said with a little smirk. "Surely you've realized that it's a one way door out there."

"Oh yeah, the door. The one with all the strangle symbols and magick woven around it," Charley said. "I hadn't seen one like it before, so I left it standing open when I came in. You could ask Agent Simmons to verify, but I'm afraid he's busy... counting some razor sharp dragon teeth. There's a lot of them, I'd hate for him to lose count midway."

Smiling at the expression that came to his face, Charley moved closer, placing both hands on the desk and leaned forward. "Perhaps you'd like to continue this in private."

"Cat got your tongue?" Charley asked, reaching out and picking up the crystal from the desktop. "Shame it isn't glowing, I don't have a small one like this in my collection yet."

"Ah," Charley said slowly as the distant sound of thunder was heard. "It wasn't your face I'd seen before, it was your talent. You're the one who tried to get me when Anna and I were going into my house that day... you sent a lightning bolt at me."

"Don't touch that, you don't what that is," Harold snarled, his face twisting up as he watched Charley examine the gemstone again. "Little girls shouldn't play with dangerous toys."

"The little red haired girl is growing up, Harold," Charley replied, looking up at him once more. "I hear you've been naughty. You know what my presence means, the balance must be restored."

"It's not me that you want," Harold slowly gave out, his eyes lingering on the dark stone she still held before glancing up at Charley, "I've never met your mother, I swear. He's the one you want, he told me what to say should you ever show up here. He made me use the lightning."

"He?" Charley asked, taking a step back with the crystal still in one hand, "He who?"

"I've said too much," a bead of sweat running down the side of his face as he turned to the agent. "Get her out of here. Do it now if you want my assistance in the next election. You can't win without my help, and you know it."

"I think I'll just wait and watch, let the voters take care of the election this time," Rodgers finally said, looking from one to the other. "Last time I had a automobile engine get thrown through the wall next to my head... and my boss thought I was on drugs."

"The fire that followed burned down the walls, so it was difficult to prove what I had written in the report."

"Here," Harold said, dropping a hand down into an open drawer of the desk, tossing several bundles of cash on the desk. "There's about ten thousand, and plenty more where that came from," he said, pushing his chair backwards and reaching back to stop himself against the wall. "You can keep that briefcase you brought for me as well."

"Listen, First Team, or whatever you're calling yourself these days. You're just some teenager following a twisted fantasy," Harold said, looking at Charley when no one moved towards the cash. "You can't handle someone who can fight back," he added as he pushed against a dark wooden panel, suddenly throwing himself through the opening that silently appeared beside him.

"Damn. Jaradan, he's headed your way," Charley sent out, moving around the desk to the opening. *Ryuu*, fun time's over. Meet us outside on the patio with May and Summer."

"What on earth is going on here?" Rodger asked as Charley stopped briefly at the hidden passage before quickly following. "He's going to come out at the fireplace, go down the hallway and cut him off," Charley called back, continuing her pursuit. "I'm following him."

"You insignificant little maggot," Amber hissed, showing a look of disgust on her face as she moved closer to the hapless

Harold, watching as he scrambled to regain his feet while exiting the narrow fireplace passageway. "The master was right, you've become a liability to us."

"This is not my doing, the trap was supposed to take care of her," Harold cried out, reaching out to steady himself as he stood up, glaring over at Amber. "He was the one who failed. I did my part."

"It's best you flee while you can, perhaps you can explain that to him when he finds you," Amber said, taking a few steps back away from him as Charley could be heard coming up behind him.

"That twisted Harold went that way," Amber let out with a slight slur to her words as Charley stood up and looked around for her prey. "I think he's headed for the patio," pointing the direction with her empty glass, letting out a little yelp as *Ryuu* brushed her aside in passing.

"He's gone to ground somewhere," Charley said, looking around the patio area as another deep rumble of thunder passed overhead.

"He can't fly," Jaradan said, carefully landing on the rail and leaning over to peer down. "Well, what do you know, there's somebody on the outside of the railing, hanging on with his hands."

"Watch out," May yelled, as *Ryuu* threw herself in front of Charley with a fast sweep of her wings, taking the full brunt of the lightning bolt that had been aimed for Charley's head before sliding down the tiles of the patio, sending the chairs in her path scattering with a loud clatter on the tiled flooring.

"Holy cow!" Simmons yelled out, partially blinded by the blast of light, unable to see what was happening. "What the hell was that?"

"Jaradan," Charley called out, "Try and grab him, let's put

an end to his little games. I want some answers."

"That tingled," *Ryuu* said, shaking herself as she regained her footing, "I feel like cooking something."

"I'm dead anyway," Harold screamed, eluding the gargoyle's grasp by leaping over to another portion of the railings. "He'll make sure of that, just ask Amber," he added with a quieter voice, sending a furious glance her way as he ducked another attempt from Jaradan.

"I don't think he's wants to talk to us," *Ryuu* remarked, looking over to Charley, before giving Amber another glance. "Maybe we'll have better luck talking to the girl. We'll apply some heat."

"Yeah, I hear they scream louder when you do that," Charley replied, following *Ryuu*'s look.

"Okay, he's all yours," Charley said out loud, giving her a thumbs down gesture as she nodded back towards Harold. "Let's all sit down with this other one who knows all about him and his boss, the one who thinks Harold's a maggot."

"You aren't talking to me or anyone else, you little bitch," Amber called out, tossing her glass to one side as she backed away from Charley, bringing herself up against the corner of the railing. "*He* won't let you."

"Oh?" Charley let out, showing a smile as *Ryuu* send a stream of fire along the length of the rail, stopping only a foot short from where Amber was cowering. "He didn't seem to mind losing Harold," leaning over to watch him fall as he caught aflame and let go, sending out a wail of terror as he fell towards the sidewalk below. "What's makes you think you're going to treated any better there, honey bun?"

"Hey, everybody just hold on here," Rodgers called out, waving a hand in the air to get everyone's attention.

"It's the law," May said, raising an eyebrow as Simmons

joined him, still rubbing at one eye to clear the tears caused by the brightness of the lightning.

"What is that?" Simmons said in awe, finally seeing the gargoyle perched on the railing in front of them.

"Just one of those things that go bump in the night, I'm sure you've heard of them," Charley replied, keeping her attention on Amber. "When I spoke with you earlier, I thought you were strange, as if something had bleached you on the inside, no evil to be noticed… no good either, now that I think on it."

"I hadn't realized that could be done," Charley added, taking a few steps closer, causing Amber to shift further back against the railing. "Guess I need to pay more attention from now on."

"What did you do, offer up your soul?"

"I've been helping poor Harold spend all that money he bilked from those saps," Amber retorted, showing a twisted smile. "I loved every minute of it, too."

"See what you guys have been dealing with," Charley said, turning to Rodgers. "Kind of makes you sick to your stomach… all those families who've lost their life's savings, no college… nothing for a rainy day… and the government lets it happen because they were getting some of the dividends."

"Power corrupts," Summer added as she passed the two agents to join her sister. "May grabbed the cash on the desk. I found some other goodies," she said, setting down a briefcase to hold up the glowing crystal with one hand as she looking over to Charley. "Look, I got this one from the mantle in there for you."

"Thanks, this one's dead," Charley said, tossing the small crystal she had been holding over to May.

"No, it's not," May said, easily snagging it with one hand. "It works just fine, but I only saw it when the lightning was about to hit you."

"It's a inner dark purple glow, so maybe that's why you didn't notice, too busy ducking."

"One type glows when you are near, and the other only in the presence of dark magickal powers," Jaradan said. "Now that might come in handy."

"Yeah," Charley said, thinking on it, "Harold must have had it laying around to let him know if his boss showed up unexpectedly. You're right, that could be a nice thing to have around."

"Now," she said, as Jaradan reached over, grabbing Amber around her waist with one hand as *Ryuu* shifted her position and snarled to distract her. "Let's hear what you have to say… starting with the name of your boss."

"I told you, I'm not talking," Amber replied, giving the gargoyle a sneering look. "Look at who you're with, she couldn't deal with a broken nail," looking back over at Charley, "So what does that say about what's going to happen to you."

"Let's hold her out over the sidewalk while we talk," Charley said out loud, while walking over to the rail. "She looks like the type that might heave when you tighten your grip."

"She's certainly full of something, that goes without saying," *Ryuu* added. "If I were you, I'd hold her out as far away from you as I could."

Chapter Seven

"Finder's keepers," May said, noting Anna's raised eyebrow at what she was holding.

"I heard you let one go," Anna said, dropping some paperwork down on her desk to look over at Charley.

"Yeah... well, you had to be there," Charley finally let out, shrugging her shoulders as she looked back at Anna.

"Look, you weren't supposed to get involved with the government this time. They should have been gone by the time you arrived," Anna said, leaning back in her chair. "Now their boss is considering therapy for those two."

"Would *you* believe they were involved with some huge monstrous looking gargoyle creature," she asked in return, "a fire breathing dragon, and two girls that for some strange reason they thought were vampires?"

"On top of that, they reported some red headed teenage girl was playing leader of the pack."

"Vampires... in modern day America. What do you suppose might be next... gnomes and fairies?" Summer remarked, exchanging looks with May, "You should have told them we're not a pack. We're a team, the best you've ever had."

"We're the First Team," Charley added, reaching out to pat Summer and May on their shoulders, "The word is already out on that."

"I'm off to find Granddon," May said, showing the dark crystal in her hand, "I want to ask him about this."

"I'll go along," Summer came out with, "Maybe there's still some good looking guys to stare at around here these days. It's been ages."

"Take care, there's wolves roaming around here today," Anna called out after them. "One of them has two legs."

"What's in the case," she asked, looking over at what May had set down on their arrival.

"Tax rebate," Charley replied, "Something those government boys forgot in all the excitement. Something poor old Harold was supposed to keep, and spend from what I understood of the conversation. The girls want to go shopping with it later, seems they don't get out very often."

"The glowing crystal there is mine, it's going to my collection in the attic."

"You let her go," Anna said, turning her attention to Jaradan. "She wasn't on the list. We could have learned more."

"No… once you started to squeeze her for information, all the evil started to ooze out," Charley said, interrupting his reply. "In the end, I thought it was best that we let her go."

"All this involved my mother in some way too, didn't it?"

"It's been a late night, everyone's worn out," Anna suddenly said, picking up her papers and tapping them on the desk to align them before tossing them in a folder. "There's someone waiting to meet you, another ring bearer. He's been hanging out all evening."

"Wolf team?" Charley asked, noting the change in topic. "What's his name?"

"Jeffery." Anna said, "Once he heard how sweet and beautiful you were, he's been dying to arrange a meeting with our newest girl."

"Cold and callous is a more apt description for her, if you ask me," Jaradan said, rising to his full height to look around, "It would be best if the meeting was brief, all of us aren't into candle lit dinners and chilled wine."

"Oh, I don't know," Charley replied, turning to look over at him, "Maybe he'll offer to take me out rowing on the lake... then a steak dinner."

"Maybe he'll realize you're jailbait once he sees you, and goes back home," Anna muttered, closing the drawer to her desk as she glanced up. "He's been persistent."

"Let's go meet this lonesome, lover boy," *Ryuu* said, looking up to Charley from her position where she had been laying down on the floor. "Maybe he'll splurge, and take all of us with you. I can eat a cow if I put my mind to it."

"Probably a wolf, too." Charley let out quietly, as she looked from *Ryuu* to Jaradan. "My defenders."

"He's on the payroll, so no wolves on the menu," Anna said. "I don't understand how all of you can talk of food after what happened to those two you just left."

"Evil gets its own rewards," Jaradan muttered. "Sooner or later, what goes around comes around."

"Karma. We just helped," Charley added, following *Ryuu* glance towards the hallway. "Plus, we were up on the patio at twenty stories or so, and they landed way down there on the sidewalk. No big deal."

"Hey, guys," May called out as they rounded the corner, "Look who we found roaming the halls back there."

"This is Jeffery, he's a twenty something," Summer remarked, smiling at Charley's expression as they walked him up to her. "He's just a little pale still... we're thinking he's studying to be an orthodontist, he kept staring at our teeth."

"It's probably that brightening toothpaste we started using,"

May said, giving out a wide smile to display her pointed teeth.

"Where's his wolf?" Charley asked, examining Jeffery's ashen appearance.

"Ran back that way, boss." May sighed, gesturing towards the hall, "Probably cowering under Granddon's desk as we speak."

"Hey, I'm Charley," reaching out to take one of Jeffery's hands in greeting. "I see you've met some of my team, over there is Jaradan and *Ryuu*," Charley said, turning to point the others out to him. "You'll have to excuse my appearance," noting how Jeffery's eyes widened at the sight of her top. "We've just gotten back from a mission, so I haven't had time to go back to casual yet."

"I think he needs some water or something," *Ryuu* said after a moment.

"Yeah, maybe some fairy dust," Jaradan added, exchanging looks with *Ryuu*, "Of course... maybe this is his normal condition."

"Looks like he's going to faint on you," Anna said, keeping an eye on the group. "Go find a place for him to sit down. The girls must of scared him."

"Hey now, it wasn't me who jumped out of the shadows and growled," May quickly let out, looking over to her sister.

"Couldn't have been me, I don't growl," Summer replied, showing a smile. "Must be his nature."

"Well, something seems to have scared the poor boy half to death," Charley said. "Maybe he's just shy around us girls," looking over to Anna.

"Hey, we could take him swimming, that might fix him up," Jaradan suggested, sitting back down. "We can bring the girls along, they haven't been there yet either."

"Perhaps he should get some rest, he wasn't looking like

that before you and the wild bunch showed up," Anna said, giving Jeffery another look. "Something's wrong with him."

"May, where did you find him?" Charley asked, raising an eyebrow.

"Granddon's office, he was in there sneaking around when we arrived," May replied, shrugging her shoulders. "We didn't growl or anything."

"Why did you go there in the first place," Anna asked, leaning back against her desk to face them.

"The other crystal, we're having a piece of it set into a pendant for the boss," Summer said. "It's a kind we haven't seen before, it has this weird kind of glow to it."

"What are you thinking, some sort of radiation poisoning?" Jaradan asked, rising up and moving closer to Jeffery.

"Possibly, he did tell me it was a dangerous toy," Charley replied, keeping her attention on Jeffery's reaction. "Let me try something for a moment," as she walked over and reached out to touch each of them.

"Ah, the roof," Jaradan let out, turning to face the winds, "Feels great. The moon is just rising. Nice view."

"Just take some deep breaths," Charley said, keeping her eyes on Jeffery. "Let me know if there's any improvement."

"I think the air is helping," Jeffery finally let out after a minute. "Boy, I thought I was going to fall over there for a moment."

"Yeah, us too," Charley said, still keeping her eyes on him. "Any idea on what caused this?"

"No, I was just checking out some of the vials on the shelf, and some girls came in. After that, it begins to get a little hazy." Jeffery replied haltingly, dropping his gaze back down to Charley's top. "That's about all I can recall."

"Your thoughts?" Charley asked, turning towards Jaradan,

"Just some BS on his part... vying for my attention, or is there something real going on here. He seems to be recovering out here."

"Could just be a bad case of instant puppy love," Jaradan replied, giving the boy another glance, "Or lust... if you take in his age and repeated interest on your state of dress."

"Is there a cure for that sort of thing?" Charley asked, still thinking on possibilities.

"Sure, grab him by his feet and hang him out over the sidewalk," Jaradan said, giving out a slight laugh. "It cures most things, for awhile anyway."

"I suppose you could just leave him up here after that," he added. "Let him find his own way back inside."

"Yeah, however, there is still the possibility of it having something to do with that new type of crystal the girls had with them," Charley said, looking back to Jeffery. "Since you're feeling so much better, how about we go back inside and see if it returns."

"Wait, just a minute," Charley suddenly said, raising a hand towards Jaradan as she peered over at Jeffery. "Something just came to me when I saw the moon beginning to show... Anna said you're Wolf team..."

"Jeffery, you sneaky thing. You're a werewolf... aren't you?"

"Does Anna know?"

"I don't need to tell you anything," Jeffery retorted, giving Charley a wave with one hand as he took a step back away from them. "You're no one special, just some stuck up kid. The way everyone was going on about you, I thought you were older... more mature. I'll be leaving now."

"Want to see mature?" Charley asked, raising an eyebrow.

"Alright, I'll tell you, I'll tell you," Jeffery wailed, holding himself away from the side of the building with his arms whenever Jaradan swung him against it. "Just let me up."

"About time, my arm was getting weak," Jaradan muttered, looking over to Charley. "I guess I'm worn out from those two earlier."

"Oh yeah, sure you are. You just wanted to let him go," Charley said, peering down past Jeffery's nervous face. "Whose vehicle is that down there. Any idea?"

"No," Jaradan replied, following her glance down towards the street below, "Bummer if it's Anna's. She'll have to go clean it now."

"If she asks about it, we can all just point at Jeffery," he added, setting Jeffery down on the roof top, dropping his legs down with a thump. "We haven't even eaten our supper yet."

"Well, it's not what you think," Jeffery began with, looking from Charley over to Jaradan as he recovered. "I have this condition, that's all. Granddon was helping me out with some special powders."

"Ask the two girls that showed up, he was out in his storeroom, looking for an spare vial for me to use. I stop in once a month and pick one up. Since I'm scheduled to be away, I asked if he had an extra one."

"You're keeping it hidden from Anna, is that what I'm picking up here?" Charley said, crossing her arms while she waited on an answer.

"Come on Jeffery, it's getting late and almost my bedtime," Charley said, raising an eyebrow. "Spill it."

"Yeah, she just thinks I'm good with wolves. I can get them to do by bidding, so to speak," Jeffery replied, trying to sooth his nerves by rubbing his hands down the sides of his legs, "I answered this ad one day and got offered a job.

Granddon picked up it right away, so he's been helping me with various charms, some different potions that prevent me from changing."

"I'm not a bad person, I just have this problem that I'm learning to deal with."

"A werewolf might be seen as a magickal creature, he's certainly not evil," Jaradan offered up, looking over to Charley. "The crystal might have had some effect... perhaps it can nullify whatever Granddon was using."

"Perhaps it can nullify a lot of things," Charley mused, "We don't know what effect, if any, it might have had on the lightning bolt since *Ryuu* stopped it."

"The girls did say it had a dark glow to it, perhaps it was just beginning to have an effect," Jaradan replied. "However, it hasn't seemed to affect you, we arrived back here without any problem. You were the one carrying it."

"Maybe I'm not magickal," Charley replied. "Maybe I'm something else."

"Look, I'm sorry about the comments earlier," Jeffery suddenly came out with. "How about we start over, maybe we can go out on a date tomorrow. We can get to know each other."

"How about we hold him out there for another five minutes, I think the wolf side is beginning to emerge again," Charley said, giving Jaradan a glance. "He's not cured yet. I'm going to head home for a sec and change."

"It took him a few minutes longer than expected, but he's feeling better," Charley said, looking over to Anna as they reappeared next to *Ryuu*.

"I used the time to change," setting one foot up on a nearby chair to finish tying her shoelace.

"He still looks pale to me," Anna said, giving Jeffery her attention.

"I think it was something I ate on the way over here," Jeffery let out, nodding his head at the remark, looking around at everyone. "Yeah, I'm sure that has to be it. Maybe I should just go back to my motel and get some rest."

"Why don't you just have Charley take you back home," Anna suggested. "You can stop by later and pick up your car."

"Oh, no," Jeffery quickly replied, holding up one hand at the remark. "I'm sure she has more important things to do. I'm not here to intrude. I'll just go back and look for that lost wolf of mine, and then be on my way."

"It was nice to meet all of you," he added while turning back to give them all once last glance before leaving the office.

"A strange sort of guy," May remarked, as everyone watched as Jeffery made his way to the corridor and turn down the hallway, letting out a low whistle.

"I hope he can drive, he usually gets himself a SUV rental when he brings that wolf," Anna said, looking over to Charley.

"I think we saw it from the roof," Charley said, looking over to Anna. "It's parked out in the street down there."

"Take those when you leave," Anna said, nodding to several magazines on the table beside Charley. "They're your first fashion layouts, hot off the press. Your mom is going to go wild when she sees them."

"She's going to faint when she sees this one," Summer said, beating her sister to grab up the top magazine, stopping to stare at the first photo she came across. "Nice," she slowly let out, looking up at Charley for a second before returning her attention to the photos as she leafed through the pages, "Oh la la. What a babe."

"Well, as long as it doesn't have a fold out center page, I'll be able to explain it," Charley said.

"How?" May asked, looking up at her from the magazine. "This is quality work," she added.

"I'll think of something by tomorrow, you can help me pick out the best one to show her," Charley said looking around at the rest of her team. "It's been a long day, let's head home, guys."

"It's already tomorrow," Anna said, glancing up at the clock on the wall. "We'll all go get some rest. I don't have anything else for the time being."

"Shopping tomorrow," Summer said, reaching down and picking up the case they had brought, still holding on to one of the magazines. "I just got some ideas on what to go looking for."

"Hey, I'm home," Charley let out as she stepped through the door, her hands full of shopping bags.

"Charley, it's his birthday, not Christmas for the family," Darlene said, shaking her head at the sight of her. "Do you save any money for yourself?"

"Sure, mom," Charley replied dropping her bundles on the couch with a sigh of relief. "All of this isn't for Jamie, I decided to pick up a few items for myself while I was out there among the screaming kids. You'd think the circus was in town, some of those soccer moms can't be passed in the aisles."

"Well, once you buy yourself that new computer, you can go shopping online. You'll be needing all that school stuff," Darlene said, helping her to take boxes and clothing items from the plastic bags.

"It might be fun to ask one of your friends to go with you though, go out for ice cream and maybe a movie," she added.

"Jacob stopped by?" Charley asked, looking up at her as she brought out one of the magazines from Anna, along with other presents.

"Yes, he's been going past here on that bike of his like some lost, wandering soul," Darlene sighed, giving her a look. "You might want to stay home on the weekends sometimes, see his face at the table again."

"Here, this one's for you," Charley said, not bothering to comment on her photos. "Hot off the press."

"Hey, Jacob," Charley let out, looking up to see him approaching on his bike, the brakes squealing as usual as he slowed down to stop in front of her.

"Hey," he replied, keeping his eyes on her. "Wow, nice clothes," taking in the shorts and sleeveless top, "I thought you were still off doing your modeling thing."

"Not today, they gave me a break," Charley said, giving him a smile, "I brought you something back to look at. You don't have to read about the latest trends in fashion in these," holding out the magazine she had been holding on her lap, "My mom hasn't seen this one yet, she got another one. So don't go mentioning it in front of her."

"Wow, look at these girls in here," he sighed, sitting down beside her to open up the magazine. "All these live overseas, I guess," trying to make sense of the text.

"I imagine so," she said, grinning at his expression as he began to leaf through the pages. "This one is from France, they even mention what perfume they're wearing."

"Who care about that?" Jacob muttered, letting out another sigh as he reached the bathing suit section. "Wow."

"Well? You've stared at that one long enough, what do you think?" she asked, looking over at him.

"Wow," Jacob replied, still looking at the photo of Charley. "Can I have this one," looking over to her before turning the page to see if there was another of her.

"I like that one best," Charley said, pointing out another pose. "That suit fits me better. I like the colors."

"Who cares about the colors," Jacob let out in a whispered voice, his attention on the photo. "Man, you're looking hot."

"The shorts are next," Charley said, trying not to laugh at his expression as he hurriedly sifted the pages, looking for her.

"Oh," he let out, his eyes widening again as he found one with the short shorts. "Are you wearing anything beneath those things," he finally managed to get out, keeping his eyes on the magazine.

"I don't recall now," Charley replied, still smiling at his reaction. "Let your imagination be your guide."

"I don't think so," Jacob slowly let out, turning the page to let the sunlight hit it from another direction.

"Sorry, those shadows don't move. I think they're there for a reason," Charley said, giving him a pat on the back. "That one's yours, keep it safe, I have another copy upstairs."

"Oh, wait a minute here," Jacob slowly let out, suddenly realizing how Charley's hair covered most of her back. "That's all you're wearing. You can tell, you can see the side of your...ah..."

"Here, this goes with it," Charley quickly said, reaching down behind her legs to bring out a wrapped package. "I picked this up for you, since I was there."

"Wow," he let out, setting the magazine down to unwrap the box, bringing out a replica of the Eiffel tower. "Thanks."

"I didn't think you'd want a bathing suit," she replied, "In case you're wondering, I didn't get to meet any of the tanned French hunks on the beach, I was busy working. I picked up some perfume for myself."

"Did I tell you Walsh got grounded?" Jacob asked, reluctantly closing the box to look over at Charley.

"No... don't think I heard that," she said, trying not to laugh. "What happened?"

"Him and his little gang of friends were caught trashing the pool," he replied, giving the cover of the magazine his attention again for a moment.

"You can check out the lingerie section when you get it back home. So what happened?"

"Oh, I heard they got caught in somebody's yard, running around naked. My mom says they were trying to look into the windows," he replied, carefully replacing the magazine back in the plastic cover it had been in. "All of them got some community service to do, starting with cleaning the pool over at the school."

"Principal Johnson got involved, too. He wants them to admit what they did to all the students when we have our first meeting in the auditorium."

"Oh, that's right, school," Charley let out. "I had forgotten that's coming up. The last year we have to deal with."

"Man," Jacob suddenly said, noticing the rings on Charley's hand, "You have some nice jewelry now too, That's a dragon carved on the red one," leaning down to examine them. "It's like that statue we saw when we went over to see about that job where Walsh was asked to drop his pants. I can't wait for that to get around school. I'm going to tell everyone I know."

"I think I like the dragon better," studying the two rings as Charley held her hand out. "That other one is kind of creepy looking. Reminds me of that thing we saw up on the roof that time."

"Hey, weren't you going to get yourself a new bike this summer," Charley asked, looking over at the same old bike he had been riding for years.

"Yeah," Jacob said, giving it a glance, "Needed new clothes. I'm saving up for the prom, you know," turning to look at her. "In case someone wants to go with me, that flower thing and the suit. Everything just adds up to fast for me these days."

"How about we go shopping tonight," Charley said, eyeing the bike again. "Let's go to the Super Store."

"What for, can't buy anything," Jacob said, giving out a despondent look. "I really don't like window shopping."

"I've got some dollars left over from my last paycheck," Charley said, giving him a pat on his back. "We'll eat out tonight, too. Let's find someplace where they serve real food, none of that fast crap."

"The Steak Barn?" Jacob asked, a smile coming to his face. "That's a place we don't go to very much. You can get those big baked potatoes."

"Steak it is," Charley said, glancing down at her watch. "Let's leave at 6, that'll give time to eat and then go shopping. I'm driving, so it won't take us that long to get there."

"Hey, did you see the new TV my dad got?" she asked, looking back at him. "My mom's out showing that magazine I gave her to all her friends. Come on, we have it all to ourselves."

"Thanks for going with me," Charley said, pulling into Jacob's driveway. "I had a nice time. Guess I needed to get my feet back on the ground."

"You need some help getting that new bike out?" she asked, pushing the switch that opened the trunk.

"I'll put it together tomorrow," he said, giving a heave to set the box down. "Let's put it in the garage."

"Whose car is that?" Charley asked, looking at the banged

up sedan sitting out on the street in front of Jacob's house.

"My mom's new friend," he replied, pausing for a moment to give it a glance. "Another loser. I can't stand him. He talks rough to me all the time if my mom isn't around."

"Yeah, I think I know the type," Charley mused, looking towards the house before picking up her end of the box. "You let me know if he gets nasty."

"What are you going to do, come over here and kick his butt for me?" Jacob asked, letting out a low laugh. "That'd be a sight to see."

"Yeah, that's me," Charley said, giving him a smile. "Take a belt to his sorry ass. There's no room in this world for another bully."

"You just tell him you have friends that care," she added while he opened the garage door. "Tell him I'll come calling if he doesn't straighten up and fly right. I've heard that going wild on someone brings its own rewards. He won't like them."

"Charley, Mrs. Dennings down at the parlor wants to know if you'd model for her," Darlene said, setting her groceries down on the kitchen table as she came in. "She's trying to get the place noticed, and when I showed all of them your photos, she almost fainted."

"Which one paled the old monarch," Charley asked idly, looking in from the living room. "Me topless?"

"You?" her mother asked, walking to the doorway to look in at her, "In which one?"

"Oh, just talking in here, mom," Charley replied. "I forgot you had the upcoming Fall Edition."

"The one with a cute hat, with the leaves all around you," Darlene said, giving her a look. "She wants to use something like that for her window, the one that faces Elm street. She was surprised to learn my daughter was a model now."

"She wants to know if you'll pose for something, you know, for the business."

"Sure, mom. Set it up. Make sure you can be there, too. Maybe you can get some discount coupons," Charley replied, returning her attention to the TV.

"Oh, that a nice idea," Darlene said, returning to the table. "Did you show your photos to anyone else, dear?"

"Just Jacob, I didn't think dad was into modeling all that much," Charley said. "He hasn't seen all of them, he would have called by now."

"Oh, I forgot, he called right after you went out this morning," Darlene said, coming back over to the doorway. "Sounded like he was sick, or crying, said he couldn't come over for awhile."

"He was fine the other day," Charley said, thinking on the news. "I should give him a call."

Chapter Eight

"I know that look," Summer let out, glancing over at Charley as she appeared in front of the fireplace, "What's happening?"

"Minor evil," Charley replied, shaking her head in anger. "My friend is in need of our services. I can tell he's in a bad way, so I thought I'd grab one of you two to go along with me, before I did something rash."

"That would be me," Summer replied, glancing towards the window at the setting sun, "in about half an hour."

"We can handle minor evil," May said, entering the room. "What's the issue?"

"My friend, Jacob," Charley sighed, looking over at the pair. "He says he's sick but I can smell the evil around his house. I went to check on him but he wouldn't come down to the door. Something's happened."

"There's a light breeze in the air," May let out, grinning as her cape began to billow around her.

"Feels good," Summer said, smiling from the feeling, "Like the old days."

"Let's go in through garage," Charley said, looking at the house. "I know what's inside, we'll sneak up to his room from there."

"Oh, man," she slowly let out sighting the mangled frame of Jacob's new bike on the floor.

"Looks like he was attacked," Summer said, giving the bike a quick glance, "We should take care, the beast must be close. I'll call the house, *Ryuu* is on watch tonight."

"There's a man and a woman in the kitchen," May noted, listening to the sounds, "Someone is in pain up those stairs," exchanging glances with her sister as Summer put her cell phone away.

"Is that you? I was afraid to say anything," Jacob moaned, clutching at the covers of the bed when he opened his eyes to see the three of them watching him. "I'm sorry."

"How did you get those bruises," Charley asked, coming over beside him sitting down on the edge of the bed to examine his face, trying to hide the concern she was feeling.

"He did it," he slowly admitted, glancing towards the door, "He said he'd be back if I told."

"He saw my new bike, and wanted to know where I got the money for it. He didn't believe me when I told him it was a gift. Then he tore up my room, looking for money."

"He stole my prom money, Charley," he sobbed, a tear running down his cheek before he coughed, grabbed at his chest with a gasp of pain.

"I can smell his blood, Lady. Your friend is dying," May said quietly, looking over to Charley. "One who deals in death is not a minor evil. Time is short if you wish to save him. The dawn will find him gone."

"He's bleeding, internally," Summer added, giving Jacob a look, "We will need help."

"More help than Gretta, I think," Charley said, her face expressionless as she picked up the phone beside the bed. "I'll get an ambulance headed this way. Let's go get our evil, take him out on the front lawn. I do believe we have a fire-breathing dragon inbound. She's well qualified to take care of this type of evil."

"You think you're big stuff," he let out, gasping in pain as Summer and May tossed him down on the front lawn. "Takes two of you to sneak up on me," he snorted, spitting towards Charley while holding his side.

"A couple broken ribs, a minor issue considering what's coming," Charley said, stopping a dozen feet away from him. "I guess the girls don't know their own strength. How's it feel to be on the receiving end?"

"Where's Jacob's prom money?" she asked, "You stole it."

"Kiss my backside, honey. That was my beer money," he let out, trying to get to his knees as he faced her, "Sneaky kid lied to me, just like his mom. She's next, she just doesn't know it yet."

"I think not," Charley quietly replied, listening to the faint sound of an approaching siren, giving *Ryuu* a glance as she landed behind him with a deep ground shaking thud. "I told him I would kick your butt, but seeing him laying up there has given me a better idea."

"Let's get him downstairs, it won't hurt if we do it," Charley said, looking over to May as the screams erupted behind her, echoing off the front of the house, "Jacob's mother can explain what happened when they find what's left of the smoldering carcass."

"She's hiding in the kitchen, told us she didn't know anything was wrong," Summer said, giving a nod towards the house.

"Go ask her out, drag her you need to," Charley asked, looking over to her. "Let her take a good look at Jacob while the medics tend to him. That might be enough to pay for what her own silence has brought about."

"May and I will take of getting him down here."

"You're always near," Charley said, stopping for a moment to give the dark shadow on the roof a quick glance. "My guy."

"Hey, look at that face," Charley exclaimed, looking into Jacob's hospital room. "About time it had a smile on it."

"Come on in," Jacob said, not bothering to wave with his arm full of tubes and needles. "You just missed your mom, and Jamie."

"Yeah, she's off and running these days," Charley sighed, stopping at the end of his bed to give him a look. "I have to go pose for a photo after this, something she's got cooked up with her hair stylist. I get to keep all my clothes on this time."

"Got some good news for you," she added, giving him a smile. "There's prom money waiting for you when ya get out, it's in an envelope. I tucked it way under your mattress, next to that magazine I found hidden under there."

"I wasn't sure how much you had saved, so I managed to wrangle a $1,000 from him," frowning as he let out a groan as he tried to shift his position.

"I got this magic button for the pain," he managed to say after a moment, giving Charley a small grin, "I just have to press it and it adds something to one of these tubes."

"Sweet. Legal drugs. You'll be the talk of the school yourself, now," Charley said. "Your bike got looked at this morning. I put it back together myself, but it sort of looks like a new Moped now. The color is the same though. Your Eiffel tower is safe, too."

"Don't worry about going back home," noting his expression, "That guy got moved out, bag and baggage. Permanently," giving him a look. "He won't be back."

"You got more back than I had, a lot more," Jacob said, thinking on what she had told him. "You're good."

"I'm the best there's ever been." Charley replied, dragging over the chair that was setting beside the door.

"Did I see you in my room with a couple of nice looking babes, or was that some kind of dream?"

"Maybe. I didn't think you dated older women, Jacob," giving him a smile.

"If they look like those two, I'll date anybody," he let out, trying not to laugh.

"I just got this new cell phone and you're the first one to call," Charley gave out, giving Anna a wry smile. "What's up this time?"

"Somebody wants to meet you, again," Anna said, opening up a folder on her desk. "Just you, it's a regular type meeting this time."

"Here's a recent photo of the location, Washington. Dress pretty, for the boys. They want to meet the red haired girl. It seems they have issues."

"Those poor Fed guys?" Charley asked, giving the photo her attention for a moment. "I wonder if this is near the Washington Monument, I always wanted to go there."

"A dress would be nice," Anna added, sitting back in her chair. "Let the model side of you show up. They're expecting you at 7."

"Fat chance," Charley muttered, setting the photo back down on the desk. "Did that last time and I thought Simmons was going to lose it. Maybe those new pants you got for me, along with my gargoyle tee shirt, and I think my mother's cloak. I might need it on this one, you never know."

"The causal look," Anna said, letting out a sigh. "I suppose that's the best I can get out of you today."

"Yeah, don't feel much like playing dress up today. I had to do business with one close to home the other day, I'm still dealing with it."

"So," she let out, nodding towards the folder, "You think they have a problem that requires someone of my talents, or has their boss decided to see for himself?"

"Could be both, they're never asked for a meeting prior to any joint operation," Anna sighed. "Maybe this one's close to home, too."

"That would explain these thoughts I've been having of late," Charley said, wandering over to the sofa and dropping herself down on it. "Evil never sleeps."

"So it would seem," Anna said. "How you doing, I mean in finding yourself," giving her a look. "All of this must have an effect."

"One wild summer. Actually, once you get over the surprise aspects, it's not a bad job to have," Charley said, leaning back with a quiet sigh, "Great co-workers. You get to travel, meet new people all the time. I've been adjusting, nothing to keep me awake at night, other than trying to figure out who I am, what happened to my mother. You know, those sorts of things, Doc."

"How's the business going? Any new faces to meet?"

"You haven't met all of the old ones, yet," Anna replied, giving her a thoughtful look, "We cover a lot of territory. They're all aware you're back with us."

"I'm not going to wet myself if I come face to face with a Ghoul team, am I?" Charley giggled, laying her head back on the sofa for a moment, "How's Sandi doing?"

"All better, Granddon and Gretta got together, gave her something extra," Anna said, looking slightly relieved that she

had shifted the topic. "She's been asking about you."
"Think she'd want to go do Washington with me," Charley asked, leaning forward to look at her. "It'd help keep those boys on their toes, and I won't have to introduce them to the ancient creatures of lore if they piss me off."
"Oh, she'd probably love it. I don't think she has many friends with that cat living with her. Makes them nervous."
"Really?" Charley asked, showing a wide smile. "I thought I was the only one who had to deal with that. Which reminds me," giving Anna her attention, "The house, any problem with me moving some stuff in there, taking over that room I found myself in?"
"You are free to do as you wish in regards to the house, it's yours," Anna said. "You might want to use your mother's old room. I understand everything is as she left it."
"Top floor, the one that faces the street," Charley said quietly. "I haven't done much exploring yet."
"That's the one, it takes up the entire front of that floor, lots of room to stretch out as I was told."
"You never went in there?" Charley asked, sitting back up.
"No… once you've explored more, you'll discover that there is no door. That's probably why you haven't thought of it before now."
"Go talk to your buddy up there in the attic, he'll know how you'd get inside. I was told you need a key."
"A key," Charley mused, showing a smile again. "A key to a door that doesn't exist. I suppose this is one of those things I'm to learn as I go along."
"Seems that way," Anna replied. "Something's take time."
"Yeah, until I turn eighteen, and inherit. What exactly is it I'm inheriting?" Charley sighed, standing back up. "Oh, yeah, wait for the reading of the will. Let me know what Sandi says,

let her know what to wear if she can make it. I'll stop back in to get the map to her place."

"Hold up," Anna said, raising a hand, before opening the desk drawer and setting a flat box down. "Your pendent is ready. Let me know if it does anything. This is something new to Granddon, he's interested."

"I see somebody likes me," Charley managed to get out as the big cat rose up, placing his paws on each shoulder as he licked her face.

"He loves you, he knows what you did," Sandi remarked, giving Charley a smile as she glanced over while she tied her shoes.

"I'm getting this boy a spiked collar for the holidays," Charley said, watching as the cat dropped down and went over to sit down next to Sandi. "He'll look like a Prince."

"Oh, he's already that," Sandi said, grinning at her. "Follow me," leading her to a back bedroom, "See?"

"Kittens!" Charley let out in surprise at the sight of the two grey cubs as they tumbled over their mother to get a look at her.

"How's the landlord dealing with all of them," Charley asked, watching as the cubs tried to attack her shoestrings.

"The Company owns the building," Sandi replied. "No rent, no fuss. I'm the landlord, too."

"Ready?" Charley asked holding out her hand, "Who knows what lurks in the heart of the city, evil knows no bounds."

"You look nice with your hair down like that. Think I'll need a jacket," seeing Charley's cloak.

"This is just for effect," she replied, resting her other hand on the soft fur on the leopard's head. "It's supposed to be nice weather there, but we might give them a chill. One never knows," as they all briefly glowed and faded.

"Fancy," Sandi let out looking around the room they found themselves in. "So this is what our tax dollars bought."

"Guess so," Charley said, nodding her head as she looking around at the antique furniture and the large paintings on the walls, "Marble floor, too."

"We must be early," she added, giving her watch a glance.

"Or, they're waiting outside," Sandi remarked, letting her cat roam the room as they made their way over to one of the padded benches. "Sometimes when you go hunting, you have to wait."

"Hey, how did you two get in here?" Agent Simmons asked, peering in from the open door. "This room was empty five minutes ago."

"We followed him," Sandi replied, nodding over towards the leopard now lying on the floor beside them.

"Magic, dark magic," Charley added, giving him a smile.

"Creature girl, no, wait," he said, stepping in the room. "It's First Team girl now, if I recall correctly," giving Charley his attention after staring at the cat for a moment.

"You must be our cat girl," Agent Rodgers said, walking in past Simmons. "I remember you from the briefing we had on that missing vial case," giving Sandi a glance.

"That's us, Ghost and Charley, from the First team," Charley said, keeping her attention on him. "You got most of it right."

"We asked you here for several reasons," Rodgers said, crossing his arms as he stood looking at them. "You two look like a couple of kids, like you got lost out there touring the mall."

"Yeah," Sandi let out, as her cat suddenly rose up, padding

quietly over to sit in front of the bench, his green eyes on the two agents. "We were just out walking this 160 pound kitty. Sorry, no leash."

"Where's that other thing," Simmons asked, checking the room again. "That one with all the teeth?"

"Home, resting," Charley replied, checking her watch again, "Is this going to take long?"

"As I was saying," Rodgers said. "We needed to show the boss that we weren't losing it, for starters."

"A single room, one way in, and out. With some other folks outside in the hallway, no doubt," Charley said, giving him a smile. "No way for the kids to get in here. Unless or course, they weren't ordinary kids."

"Send in the boss man, I'd like to see the expression on his face, and listen to how he explains how we got in here with a wild, endangered leopard. You can tell him the area is secure."

"Is it?" Simmons asked, giving the cat another look. "That beast looks hungry, it could go at somebody."

"Life is uncertain, deal with it. Sandi has everything under control," Charley said. "Is that it?"

"Where's your team?" Rodgers asked. "I didn't think you'd come alone."

"I'm never alone, Agent Rodgers," Charley replied, showing a little smile. "I have a shadow, should we need any help. I think you met him last time we got together, that time with poor Harold. He's near if we need him."

"I brought a friend, she wants to do Washington with me after this meeting you asked for."

"I see," Rodgers let out, pursing his lips. "How about we all go upstairs, there's a couple of folks waiting to meet you. They have a few questions to ask."

"Nice," Sandi said, pointing out the life size statues they

passed on the way. "How do they know what they looked like?" giving Simmons a questioning look.

"From painting's, I suppose," he replied. "I never gave it much thought," he added, giving a shrug of his shoulders.

"They guessed," Charley said, giving the closest one a glance as they went past. "Who's to know the difference 200 years later?"

"In here," Rodgers suddenly said, opening the door to lead them into another room.

"Here they are, sir," he announced, looking at one of the two waiting men, "As I said, they were downstairs."

"Cloak and dagger?" Sandi asked, giving the older one her attention, reaching down to place her hand on top of the cat's head as he sat down between them.

"Here we are," Charley said showing a raised eyebrow as she placed her hand on top of Sandi's. "You had a question for me?"

"I'll get right to it," the older man said, giving both of them an appraising look. "Frankly, I haven't believed much of what's been reported. However, I'm unable to get those two to change their story. So, I'm forced to accept that there's something to it," giving Charley another look. "You're the red haired girl, the one I keep hearing about?"

"None other," Charley replied, keeping her eyes on him. "You seem to have a problem with something. Do you want that something dead?"

"I need some proof," he replied, "Convince me you're the one, before we sit down and have our little talk."

"I don't change colors, or anything like that," Charley told him. "We're sort of limited on show and tell. How about you contact the Agent nearest to the Lincoln Memorial and ask him if there's a new statue on the roof. Have him check the side that faces this building."

"It'd be quicker if you had some binoculars, just take a peek across the pond out there."

"It's a reflecting pool," Simmons said, giving them a look. "You don't swim in it."

"Wanna bet," Sandi let out quietly, raising an eyebrow as they exchanged looks.

"Enough games, I'm not into statues, they're a dime a dozen around here," the older man said, waving a hand at Simmons. "Show me something more than this tame, toothless leftover from the circus here," nodding at the cat.

"Ready to go shopping?" Charley asked, turning her head to look over at Sandi. "I don't like the reception they laid out for us."

"Yeah," Sandi replied, nodding her head slightly. "Rude folks here in the big city. They didn't even have those finger chicken sticks I like to dip in my mustard," she added. "Let's head out."

"This place reeks," Charley said, giving Rodgers her attention. "I don't mean that old stale smell from all those politicians reaming the rest of us over the years, something bad walks these halls. Be warned."

"We're going to go grab a bite to eat, then maybe go girl shopping," Charley said, giving the older man a look. "Go call somebody else, try that psychic hot line. Try to be polite, it helps."

"Oh, Agent Simmons," Charley said, turning towards him for a moment. "There's something wading this way across that pond out there, and it's about nine feet tall. You can't stop it, so don't bother him. He's with us."

"We're heading over to the Washington monument for a minute. Thanks for the invite, and showing us around, Mr.

Carlson, Director of the FBI," she let out, before giving him a quick wave with her free hand as they vanished.

"Get all the pigeon goo off?" Charley asked, trying not to laugh at Jaradan's expression as he lifted himself onto the sidewalk beside the reflecting pool.

"Almost stepped on a duck," he muttered, stamping his feet to shed the water, "or maybe it was a midget swan, I couldn't tell. Too damn dark out here, this is a scary place after the sun sets."

"No matter, we had our own experience with the strange and eerie ourselves, we met someone else from the FBI," Charley said, leading him over to the nearest streetlight, giving his feet a look. "You seem to be free of it."

"A shape changer," the gargoyle muttered, stamping his feet once more, sending several widening cracks down across the cement, "Oops. Sorry."

"It wasn't one of the men we met," Sandi said, looking up at him, "but you're right, it has that scent."

"Let's stroll over towards that tall looking obelisk," Jaradan said, remembering Charley's interest, "Maybe I can sit on the top. Air dry myself."

"It comes to a point up there," Charley let out, with a quick laugh. "I don't think that'd be very comfortable, but then again, I'm not a gargoyle."

"Fortunately for the rest of us," Jaradan replied, his smile evident in his tone.

"They weren't very nice to us," Sandi said, giving him another look as they made they way towards the monument. "I thought we handled ourselves pretty well under the circumstances."

"Damn, that didn't take long," Charley let out as her cell phone began to buzz. "Must be Anna."

"Chuck it in the pond," Jaradan said, giving the device a glance, "Can't be calling just to ask about the weather."

"Maybe it's a new mission," Charley said, looking at the phone as the noise continued.

"We just had one, it wore me out," Sandi said. "I say we're off the clock."

"They were rude to us," Charley said, finally opening the phone and speaking into it, "Tell them to kiss my ass, and then go to hell," she then added, after listening for a few minutes to what Anna was saying.

"She says they're coming over to say 'sorry'," looking over to Sandi as she put her phone away. "Over at the needle."

"I guess they want something dead after all," giving Jaradan a glance. "We better hurry up if you still want to sit up there for a few minutes. That's where they're headed. The breeze from the top should dry you off in a couple of minutes."

"Damn Feds," Sandi sighed, shaking her head. "Toothless my ass."

"Think we should go back for our battle armor?" Charley asked, looking upwards as Jaradan swiftly moved upwards with heavy flutters on his wide wings.

"Maybe the girls," Jaradan muttered, trying to perch himself on the granite top. "We can cover more area. I think they can smell blood at least a mile away, a shape changer should be easy prey."

"Good point, I'll be right back," Charley said, looking over to Sandi. "If he falls, just give him a kick to his backside after he gets back up on his feet."

"Got it," Sandi grinned. "I hope he does," as Charley vanished with a glimmer.

"Damn, she's already got reinforcements," Simmons let

out peering out the window at the group waiting for them as he stopped the car.

"There's definitely something strange about those other two," Rodgers said, taking in the gowns, their dark hair running down their cloaks in thick waves. "They look like they're off a cover of one of those paperback novels."

"Nice cleavage," Simmons sighed, "I like the whole vamp look they've got going on. I've always like girls with dark eyes like that."

"Say something rude to us again, and I'll have your car put up there on the very top," Charley said, slowly walking over to the vehicle, to stand facing them with arms crossed. "I think you know I can do it, and have it spin around, too. Try and explain that, after you walk back."

"We won't have to knock over a hotdog stand later to feed my toothless kitty, either," Sandi let out, giving them a disgusted look. "He'll munch on Grade A government ribs. It only takes one of you to report your failure."

"Ah, look girls, he's got a lot on his plate," Rodgers said, stepping out to walk around to the front of the car, leaning back against it as he gave them all a look.

"We're after something, and we don't even know what's really going on," looking to Charley, "Some of our people have been found in a coma, but others swear they've seen them over at their office just minutes before. They've even signed into the visitor log. Things are getting confused."

"We're afraid someone's trying to infiltrate the government, using some elaborate disguise," Simmons said, joining him. "We don't think anyone's walking around wearing a mask. So, we asked to have the boss meet with you. We figured you'd have some ideas for us."

"Interesting," Charley mused. "You guys have a infestation

problem. Somebody from the dark side is trying to do some dealings, using your own people to do it. I have an excellent idea on what you're dealing with but you won't like it," giving each of them her usual look.

"I'd tell those Secret Service boys to keep their eyes on the man," Sandi added. "He's a likely target."

"Yeah, we figured that," Rodgers said, looking over at her, "so he's under a 24 hour visual. He's hating it, but values his life a bit more than his privacy."

"We can't watch them all."

"So we came to mind," Charley said, slowly smiling at their discomfort. "I could spend the rest of my life dealing with the little wildfires these people start around here, the petty bickering, stabbing each other in the back as they smile at the nearest camera. It might not be pure evil, but it's close enough to get my attention, and show my disgust."

"Just the one we want," Simmons said, holding up a hand. "That's it. We'll keep an eye on the rest of them."

"Let them take out each other," Sandi said, smiling at the thought. "Maintain the *status quo*."

"It works, no sense rocking the boat," Simmons replied, beginning to look uncomfortable as the leopard let out a little noise while showing all his teeth, its eyes on him.

"Poor boy, he's getting hungry," Sandi said, reaching down to rub the side of the cat's head, giving Simmons a look.

"You can't afford my services," Charley finally said, shaking her head at Rodgers. "We don't work for rude people. We're just a couple of nice young girls, out taking in the sights of the city."

"That's May and Summer, over there," nodding to the waiting pair. "Team girls. In case we encounter some muggers along the way. They hope to reduce the surplus population, if we draw any out of hiding."

"You guys are so screwed," Sandi said, showing a sad face for them, "We were there for all of 15 minutes. If you had been polite, we would have told you what you're up against, and might have said how to deal with it."

"As it turned out, the boss man decided to treat us the same way I suspect he treats you two," Charley said. "There's no place for a non-believer among us, guys. Tell him to find some faith. We work as a team, we don't take prisoners, and we don't work for free."

"You're not going to help?" Simons asked, his eyes widening as the revelation came to him.

"Do I look like I'm in the mood?" Charley asked, giving him her fixed look for a moment.

"Ah... no," he replied, glancing over to Rodgers. "He isn't going to like that."

"I was told he was coming here to apologize," Charley said, placing a hand on one hip as she looked at them. "I don't see his sorry ass. That's two snubs in one evening, it's a bit much. We're the sensitive type."

"Go back and tell him we could have taken care of this mess you have going on, and he decided us kids weren't the ones. Maybe I should have dressed up like Joan of Arc, and rode up the steps of the place he's hiding in on a white stallion, banner waving from the end of my lance."

"Then again, I don't have a lance, maybe that's part of his problem."

"Tell the ones over at the White House that time isn't on their side," she added, looking at Rodgers. "It'll only be a matter of time before it gets to one of the guys that goes in and out on the day to day business. You'd have to quarantine him. Good luck with that."

"Wait," Rodgers let out as Charley turned away, her

attention on the top of the monument. "What do you want?"

"Two of the largest and best blueberry pies known to exist in the city, and they better be still warm from the oven," Charley quickly replied, facing him again. "Along with a face to face honest apology. I want May in the White House. Unfettered, no questions, no one bothers her. She's a true vampire of the first order, so no one goes playing your silly government games with her or they'll pay the price. She likes to snap their spine in half first, that way she doesn't have to chase them down once they realize what she is. She's earned the respect due her. She'll advise if it comes that way."

"Summer and I will form up, and Ghost team will track this thing down. Once we locate it, we kill it, by any means it takes."

"We have total access to any place we want to check out, no one says restricted access to us or we pack up and go home. Anyone who stands in my way is considered suspect, and working for the other side. I'll have them killed just for practice."

"Mess with me, or my team, and the dome gets a hole for ventilation. There's a big parking lot out there, so don't press your luck. Don't go waving the flag, I don't vote. Understood?"

"I forgot, you need to check with that one back in the office," Charley sighed, walking over to Rodgers and grabbing his arm, "Here," giving him a little push towards the Director, who glanced up from his desk with a startled expression on his face. "Explain the situation."

"Give Simmons a call. Piss me off one more time, Carlson, and I'll use you as monster bait," she let out, giving him a dark look as she vanished from the room.

"Think he'll go for it?" Sandi asked, glancing over at her as she returned, before returning her attention back to her cat that had moved towards Simmons, sitting down to face him.

"Maybe. I'm not holding my breath," Charley remarked, raising an eyebrow as she watched the cat creep a couple of feet closer to Simmons.

"You got family, Simmons?" she suddenly asked, giving him a serious look. "Wife? The kids waiting to be tucked into bed?"

"Ah, no. Just me. Had one once, not a wife but a girlfriend," he said, showing a bead of sweat on the side of his face as the cat moved another foot closer, "She left last year, didn't like my hours."

"So, you won't be missed," Sandi remarked, showing a grim smile as the cat showed off his teeth again.

"We're cool with each other. Right?" he asked, trying to back up against the front of the car, giving them a worried look.

"About time you got back down here," Charley said, looking over at the gargoyle as he landed with a deep thud beside her. "This here is Agent Simmons, he's a lonely guy. He's suddenly looking a little nervous, too."

"I'll keep an eye on him," Jaradan said, giving the hapless agent a glance as he rose up to his full height.

"He'll keep you company," Charley said sweetly, looking over to Simmons with a smile, "We're going to walk over and check out the monument while we wait on a reply."

"You can see the entire place from the top," Jaradan said, looking over at Charley as she and Sandi started off.

"I'll let you know if I'm that interested," Charley replied, shaking her head at the thought.

Chapter Nine

"This type of shape changer is somewhat like an illusionist," Charley replied, looking around the office they were ushered into before returning her attention to Carlson, "It can take the shape of it's victim and even accomplish some of the minor aspects, same signature, recent memories, that sort of thing. It can't maintain it for any length of time though."

"At first glance, you think you're talking with the real person."

"Your man said the victims were found in a coma, that narrows it down," Sandi said, glancing over as Simmons entered carrying two pie boxes. "The worse kind eliminate them, as they replicate them."

"That would get some attention," Rodgers remarked. "We'd know it was here a lot sooner."

"Exactly," Charley said, smiling as the pies were set on the table and opened up. "So you don't really know how long it's been here, or what its master has in mind. Washington works around the clock, so copying someone while they slept and showing up at the office in the middle of the night is no big deal, unless your one of those reporters that work around here."

"Its master?" Carlson asked. "You mean someone else is involved here?"

"Sure is," Charley replied, showing Simmons the size of

pie slice she wanted, using her hands to illustrate. "That's the one we really want. We'll keep an eye out for him as we go around looking for his creature, but he'll know we're around before long. He has some talent of his own if he's teamed up with what we're after."

"What about this other one," Simmons asked, pointed at the second pie box.

"Oh, just take that out of there and open that window there," Charley said, seeing everyone had a slice. "Just rest it on your palm, no need to lose anything you might want to use later."

"Like this," he asked, looking over from the window, suddenly letting out a scream as the pie was snatched from him, nearly dragging his entire arm out the window with it.

"Yeah, you're getting hang of it," Charley replied, exchanging smiles with Rodgers. "A pie a day keeps the witch doctor away."

"You've made arrangements for May?" she asked, looking over at Carlson as she ate her pie. "It's active, I can feel it."

"I'd mark anything thing as suspect if it was generated by one of the victims," she added, "We don't know what the purpose of all this is, but I can assure you, it's not here to play nice."

"I need to be there when your girl gets set in place," Carlson said, nodding towards May. "You just can't show up unannounced. They're already a bit antsy over there."

"Let's take care of that first then," Charley let out, looking down at her shirt as he brushed off the crumbs. "There, all ready."

"The hunt is afoot," May said, walking over to stand next to her, "I'm ready."

Taking her hand, Charley reached out to touch Carlson's arm. "Here we are," she said, looking up at the startled agents standing outside the White House doors. "Do you want to tell them, or should I?"

"You said these guys that were discovered signed in, were over in one of the wings of the Capitol, so lets go over to where they were," Sandi said, looking at Rodgers. "We'll pick up the trail from there."

"We play for keeps, Rodgers. No trying to keep it for study," Charley said, as she reached back behind herself to bring out her weapon, racking the slide back to chamber a round. "It dies when we catch up to it. I don't care what the boss might have told you," replacing her gun on her belt.

"Here we are," Charley whispered, releasing her hold on Rodgers, the others letting go as Sandi looked around them. "This place looks like a library," she muttered, "lots of places to hide."

"Research library," Rodgers said quietly at her quizzical look. "We're down two levels, beneath street level."

"It was here, but the scent is old," Sandi said, waving a hand as she began to follow her cat. "It went this way."

"Creepy looking place, not much going on in here," Charley let out quietly, glancing around the shadows as they followed the cat, "What's down here," looking over at Simmons.

"The secrets of the universe," he replied, giving a shrug. "The 12 step program for making your own nuclear bomb in your basement, that sort of stuff."

"Sounds like a whole lot of trouble if it was handed over to the wrong sort of people, almost like that vial that went missing," the idea coming to her. "Maybe we're dealing with the same folks."

"Sounds reasonable," Rodgers replied, listening to what she was saying. "He's back for more, something just as deadly no doubt."

"I'm guessing they keep worst of them in there," Sandi said, nodding towards the large vault looking door before them. "The trail goes that way. He's been around here lately."

"We need an access card," Rodgers let out, sighing in frustration. "We don't have one."

"I've got one," Charley said, sharing the image of the door with Jaradan, "But once we're done, you'll be needing a new door."

"This thing is ancient," Summer pointed out, examining the door. "The damn thing weighs a ton, but it's just sitting on those hinges."

"We can lift it up, no need to go shopping for a new one," Sandi said, nodding her head as she had her cat move back away from the steel door. "Let's give him some room to work."

"Holy hell," Rodgers let out as Jaradan appeared with Charley at his side.

"Keep in mind that if it's still in there, it can look like anyone," Charley said, bringing out her weapon. "Use me or the leopard as your guide, we'll know it when it shows itself. It's close, I can tell."

"No telling how it'll react though," Sandi let out as Jaradan stepped up to the door, grasping each side with his hands and gave out with a mighty groan.

"Man, somebody has gas," Charley said, waving a hand before her face as she took a step back, "Blueberry is my guess," as he stood up, lifting the heavy door off it's hinges.

"It's only two tons, where do you want it?" Jaradan asked, giving Charley a wry glance at the blueberry comment. "It tasted good going down," he let out in a whispered tone, "I kept the plate, we can use that again later. Gretta will give me a kiss."

"Not if she smells you coming first," Charley muttered

quietly, showing him a wry grin.

"Have him sit it over there, against that wall," Rodgers said, pointing. "Maybe we can get him to put it back once all this business is finished."

"Oh, it's in there alright," Charley said, giving Sandi the nod to proceed, "Keep alert."

"What in the name of all that's holy is going on out there," a deep voice let out as they rounded the third aisle of books.

"Damn, that's the Vice-President's voice," Simmons let out lowering his weapon as they walked around one of the metal shelves, finally seeing who had spoken.

"No, it isn't," Sandi yelled out, sending in the ghost leopard to attack the creature as Charley began firing, her .40 caliber rounds hitting him in the chest with little effect as it began to change it's form.

"Aim for its head," Jaradan called out as the beast like creature let out a loud piercing scream of rage, as it swatted at the squalling cat, the papers it had been holding flying up into the air as it sought an escape route.

Still changing its shape as it hurtled itself towards the only exit, the creature took on a larger hideous image as the big cat sent it reeling sideways from the heavy blow of a paw. Recovering, it leaped aside at the cat's renewed attack, its thick curved claws tearing up chunks of flooring as it twisted around and headed towards the exit.

Leaning towards the creature, Jaradan struck it with a mighty blow as they crashed together, their growls filling the air as fists and claws flailed, each seeking to overpower the other with heavy blows, the beasts large fangs held at bay by a heavy copper bracelet Jaradan shoved in its jaws.

Finally grabbing it around the waist, the gargoyle gave out a deep, loud grunt, hurling it away from him and sending the creature flying through two aisles of metal bookshelves before it struck the far wall with a loud explosion of flying bricks.

"Where did it go?" Charley yelled out trying to circle around the books to see were it landed, her weapon held ready.

"The wall," Sandi replied, pointing out the hole in the bricks with her own weapon as she came around from the other side. "He got thrown through the bricks."

"Where does that lead to?" Charley asked, looking over to Rodgers before peering up the narrow chute that she discovered on the other side of the wall.

"It must be part of the old air shafts," Rodgers let out, running over beside to her to look up. "It has to go up to the street."

Everyone take hands," Charley called out, "*Ryuu*'s got it spotted, its headed towards the White House."

"Stand your ground, boys," May let out in her soft voice, her eyes on the distant Capitol building as she joined them out on the steps. "It's headed our way. Aim for its heart, and be aware it is very fast, and very powerful."

"We see it," one of the men on the roof called out, "Heading straight for us," as the first of the snipers began firing at it with .50 caliber rifles. "It's monstrous."

"That one's on our side," May said, holding up one hand as the others appeared down at the bottom of the steps.

"It's covered with some sort of slippery acid," Jaradan called out. "Don't touch it with your bare hands."

"Like we're going to do that," Charley said quietly, "Maybe it's flammable," watching with interest as *Ryuu* began her attack from the air, the river of fire lighting up the sky around her as the beast came into range of the men with the automatic weapons.

"We're hitting it, but it's still coming," the one on the roof bellowed down to them over the noise of the weapons. "We've knocked it down a couple times but we can't stop it with what we have up here. We need a tank, maybe two of them."

"You need the Marines. I know what to do," Charley suddenly said, giving Jaradan a quick look before focusing her attention on the creature's approach. "I know exactly what to do with this thing," taking a dozen steps out in front of them.

"Have them cease firing," she said, raising her voice to be heard over the noise as she looked over to Rodgers. "It doesn't seem to have much effect on this one. I'll take this thing on by myself."

"The crystal," May called out, pointing at Charley's new pendant. "It's come to life."

"Strange," Charley let out, glancing down at the bright purple glow that began to surround her, looking back up as the creature cleared the trees across the street from them, its entire form streaming hot vapors into the air from its encounter with dragon fire. "The bigger the threat, the brighter it glows. It's like a warning device. I guess it didn't work for Harold, he didn't know I was coming."

Pausing as it sighted the waiting team, the creature shifted its direction with a deep snarl and headed for the White House doors, the growling slobbering sounds it was emitting echoing around them as it drew closer to Charley.

Holding one hand out, Charley focused all her thoughts on the creature, showing a slight smile as she felt the energy flow through her from the earth beneath her feet as the very air around her began to shimmer and thicken. As if trapped by the density, the creature began to struggle against an unseen force to move past her, its growing screams of rage beating on their ears.

Carefully walking towards it, she reached out to touch it with one finger, wrapping the beast in a soft mesmerizing glow that suddenly flared with an intense bright blue light, leaving the air clear as it quickly faded away.

"Damn," Simmons let out. "I can't see a thing," wiping at his eyes to clear them.

"It's gone," Rodgers exclaimed, looking around the area as he put his weapon away. "It just vanished."

"Mission accomplished. We'll go take care of setting that door back in place, but you're replacing those bricks," Charley said, giving him a grin. "You guys got off easy this time, two pies and some bookshelves, a few bricks."

"The President and I watched the whole thing from up there," Carlson said, joining them as the other men were greeting them and shaking hands with her. "Well done."

"I thought you needed something dead," Charley sighed, looking over at him. "Felt it in my bones. Now you know why they called on us. Proof enough?"

"Great job, Ghost team," Charley said, giving Sandi a hug of relief. "You're getting a bonus on this one for sure."

"How on earth did you do that?" Sandi asked, keeping her voice down low. "I've never seen anything like it."

"Something somebody mentioned to me," Charley said, giving Jaradan a smile. "I wasn't sure I could do it, but I've learned to listen to what he says."

"I don't know who was behind it, there's no trace of him now," she said, looking back over to Carlson. "I think we arrived just in time, it had found what he was looking for. Maybe once you've had a chance to see what those papers in the vault were about, it'll give you a clue to his identity."

"Apparently the creature had orders to go after the President if discovered," Summer remarked, moving over to stand next to her sister. "That wasn't your everyday shape shifter, that's for sure. It was beginning to look like we were all in for a nasty battle with that thing. I thought your gargoyle was going to have to turn it inside out."

"I'm a little weak on species identification, we'll have to all sit down tomorrow and discuss it," Charley said, letting out a deep sigh. "I'm tired now. Let's wrap this up, gang. Time to go. There's a pirate movie coming on tonight that I wanted to watch."

"I don't want to know where you have that slippery acid stuff on you, so don't go trying to show me," Charley said as she held up a hand, giving Jaradan a look as he moved over next to her. "You might want to take a hot shower. It stinks, too."

"What's that?" Charley asked, seeing May holding something in her hand as Jaradan set the door back on it's hinges, Sandi directing his actions.

"Pen," May said, holding it up so everyone could see it, "My souvenir, says White House on it. They offered me something to drink while we were waiting, but when I told them I don't drink wine, they gave it to me. One of those guy's around him wanted a date. He got turned down, too much alcohol his blood."

"Hey, guys, how about we hit the showers and then go swimming, we can all go shopping tomorrow," Charley said. "I worked up a sweat over this one, and I need to relax for a bit after all this. I've got a headache."

"Good idea," Sandi said, nodding her head at the suggestion. "We're finished here."

"It was more like I suddenly remembered how to do that,"

Charley mused, giving the gargoyle a look. "Strange."

"Not as strange as watching Sandi's cat jump off the diving board," he replied, watching as the cat shook himself off before finding a place to lie down.

"I think that cat does it all, and doesn't require any blueberry pie, either," she replied, giving him another look before smiling at him. "Of course he's not as cute and cuddly."

"Why did you say aim for its head, that only pissed it off," she asked, thinking on the battle.

"How was I to know?" he asked, leaning back against the edge of the pool with a sigh. "It seemed like a good idea at the time."

"I think you knew, you wanted to goad me into action," Charley said quietly looking across the pool for a moment before looking back over at him. "You knew I'd come up with something."

"Wait a minute," looking over at Summer and May as they tried to drown each other in the deep end, "That's why those two didn't jump right in. They were waiting too."

"Everything has energy, my Lady," Jaradan said, giving her a look. "Now you have an idea on how to tap into it, whether it is a flower in your garden, or the planet itself."

"How about the universe?" Charley asked quietly, turning to give him her attention. "She could destroy the planet," thinking back on what he had told her before, letting his silence give his answer.

"That shifter was a tough nut to crack, a real nasty one," May said, grinning as she emerged upwards from the water, her dark eyes on Charley as the water streamed down her face. "We all knew you would do something, once you saw everything else was ineffective."

"She had no idea what she faced," Summer added, keeping

her voice low as she gave Sandi a quick glance. "She attacked as soon as the Lady did, no fear. I was impressed."

"We could have held it at bay, pounded on it some more, but we needed you to destroy it, otherwise it would just have returned later. It was too slippery for me to pull apart," Jaradan said, nodding his head as he looked at her. "You did good, very good."

"What is the possibility that thing was bait," Sandi asked, giving all of them a look as she walked over to sit down on the edge of the pool beside them.

"Something to draw us there," Charley said, raising an eyebrow as she considered. "If so, then the one we're after is a step ahead of us at this point."

"He gave up some of himself though," Charley said looking around at them. "He's told us his power has limitations, otherwise there would have been a dozen of those things waiting around for us."

"Maybe he didn't expect you to be so strong," Jaradan said, looking at her. "He may well take that into consideration the next time, unless he and the beast were one in the same."

"Dang, I missed my movie," Charley let out, looking at the time. "I should go tell Anna what went down before heading off to bed, and get Sandi's bonus headed her way. She's feeding those twins over at her place. She's going to need some big cow parts soon."

"Going naked?" Summer asked, giving out a smile.

"Might," Charley replied, "Quicker, and I've been told often enough how nice it makes me look."

"Wait a minute, here," Charley let out, a thoughtful expression on her face as she finally picked up her towel. "I just figured out something," giving Jaradan another look, "I've been going to school all this time, ever since I woke up after drinking that potion stuff Gretta gave me."

"The things I've been told to do were like baby steps and hints to guide me. I don't need to touch anyone or anything to get them to shift with me, I only have to think of it. Right?"

"You've got a strange expression on that face of yours… could it be guilt?"

"You've been told many times that you learn as you go. Sometimes the teacher leaves the classroom and goes straight to the lab," he said, giving her a slight shrug as he returned the look. "Sometimes it's best to go slow at first. Anyone with the ability to destroy the planet itself can appreciate the need to start off with little steps."

"It comes with a lot of responsibility as well," he added while standing up beside her, reaching down to place a hand on her shoulder. "Don't let anyone tell you otherwise. Never doubt yourself."

"You started out telling me to look behind the things I had been told, I just didn't understand until now that it applied to the things you were telling me as well."

"It just hit me… who the boss is," Charley slowly came out with, looking up at the gargoyle for a moment, before glancing around all the others gathered around her. "I should have realized it before, back when we went to go see that temple."

"You had me sit on that high throne for a specific reason," fixing her gaze on the gargoyle "That place was more than just a temple. The entire place had this strange feel to it."

"I discovered the key on my own," Charley gave out as she appeared in front of Anna's desk, trying to keep the towel around her with one hand, ignoring Granddon's sudden interest. "I didn't even need to ask him. I'm going to take a look tomorrow."

"Yes?" Anna asked, looking up at her with a raised eyebrow as she leaned back in her chair.

"Know thy self," Charley said, keeping her eyes on Anna. "Once you do, anything is possible."

"It seems we didn't need to worry over starting you off a year earlier than planned," Anna replied, letting out a sigh as she showed a thoughtful expression. "The Feds were quite pleased with the manner in which you handled their problem. I guess I can go home to bed now."

"Sure, don't stay up on my account, take tomorrow off," Charley replied, smiling at her, "I'm off to do the same, but before you leave please make a note that Sandi gets a bonus on this one. She earned it."

"Gretta stopped in to see your friend, while you were off at the wrestling match with monsters and evil persons," Anna said, taking up her pen to make a note to herself. "His energy levels have now improved, and he won't have those dreams again. She expects a complete recovery. His memory of the event is already beginning to fade away."

"You guys are good at that, hiding those memories," Charley said, showing a little smile at the thought. "You should know that sooner or later, they begin to reappear."

"Depends on what potion you drink," Anna replied, closing the folder on her desk and standing up, giving her an amused look. "Enjoy your day off, Princess. Evil doesn't sleep."

"Was that her, is she's back?" one of the operators asked, glancing over at Anna as she opened the door and entered the room, the buzz of activity enveloping her as she looked around at the other stations.

"That's her alright, she's back," Anna replied, letting out a sigh as she glanced around. "What do we have?"

"Manifestation of the third order in sector twelve," one of the other girls reported, holding one hand to her headset as she looked over to Anna. "Recon team is inbound."

"What about the portals?" Anna asked, giving the wide screen before her a glance. "I'm not seeing anything on the board."

"All portals are reporting clear," another operator called out. "The forth rings are reporting a temporal disturbance, nothing sighted, yet. The portends are reporting it as a level five threat, and caution is advised."

"Keep eyes on it," Anna said, nodding as she looked around her again. "There seems to be a lull, let's stay alert. Call me if anything major needs my attention. I've been given a day off, so Georgie can handle anything else for awhile."

"I think I might just go out on that date someone asked me about last week."

Chapter Ten

"I guess I've come a long way," Charley mused, looking down from her position on the edge of the roof, turning back to give Jaradan a brief smile before glancing up at the darkening sky as the clouds roiling over her head, "It seems so long ago though. Summer's almost over."

"The rains are coming," feeling the first drops of rain as the winds began to pick up, blowing her hair around her as she sat back down beside him, listening to the whispering of the leaves on the trees as the winds began to move them.

"It will be refreshing," he said, holding put a palm to catch one of the drops.

"Oh, I never noticed these before," Charley let out, taking one finger to rub at one of the roof tiles were one of the rain drops had landed, revealing the faint blue lines and symbols lightly etched in to the surface.

"All of them must have these," she remarked glancing around at the other tiles as other drops splattered on them, briefly displaying the ancient markings with a low glimmer of energy that rapidly faded from sight.

"Oh, we have company," following Jaradan's gaze down towards the front gate as she caught it, studying the darkly cloaked form now standing there.

"Must be one of the Portal Daemons," he finally said, keeping his eyes on the figure, "A rare sight, even for one such as myself."

"It must be important, whatever it is that brings it to my front door," Charley sighed, her eyes widening slightly as the figure glanced up towards her, the face hidden by the shadows of the hood that covered its head.

"Damn, it knows we're up here, too," she slowly added, returning the look.

"Watch," Jaradan suddenly gave out reaching out to put a hand on Charley's shoulder as she began to stand up. "You'll find this interesting."

"The damn thing is glowing," Charley finally said, watching the figure take on a subtle violet hue before it moved, stepping through the fence as if it didn't exist, the color quickly fading as it stood inside the gate with it's attention still on the pair up on the roof.

"I don't think it's come to sell us beauty products, or any Girl Scout cookies," Charley let out, giving the gargoyle another glance before returning her attention to the darkly clad form. "That thing is here for a reason. Kind of reminds me of the Grim Reaper."

"I thought you told me nothing could get past that fence. This was supposed to be my day off, and now I've got to go down there and see what's up."

"You see that sword there," Jaradan asked, nodding down at the barely noticeable hilt showing at the daemon's waist. "Probably on a Maiden's Quest."

"Yep, that's what it is," he added, watching with interest as the cloaked figure kneeled down with one knee as the bare blade, hidden by the flowing cloak, was brought out into view.

"Oh, great. A sword fight on the front lawn," Charley

muttered, giving him a look, "That's all I need."

"Watch," he replied, as the sword was carefully balanced on the one upraised knee, the other down touching the ground as the figure bowed its head in Charley's direction.

"What are the rules, I go down there and kick its butt, or do we hug like long lost family?" Charley asked, still looking down.

"It's an offer of service," Jaradan said, nodding his head, "You accept by lifting up the sword and handing it back. Kick it aside if you reject her."

"Her?" Charley asked, giving the waiting form another look. "How can you tell?"

"They are all females," he replied, "Makes it easy to guess. She's from one of the Noble Houses, you can tell from that silver pattern around the edges of her cloak."

"You're saying she's a somebody where she comes from," Charley said, now noticing the lines that he had mentioned. "What kind of quest was that?"

"To be accepted by her elders, she must serve in a position of great danger, a rite of passage," he said, looking over to Charley. "This one decided to start at the top of the lists, she came straight to you. Smart move, there is no greater danger to be found than at your side."

"That's comforting to know," Charley replied, "What's her prize if she makes it all the way?"

"They're given watch over one of the portals, the honor is beyond mere words to them."

"There is no going home if she fails," he added, anticipating the next question, "Which is why the sword is kicked aside. In their world, there is no honor in failure."

"So, she's staked all on me," Charley mused, "Her life, her entire future rests on the choice she has just made. Is that what

I'm hearing," keeping her eyes on the one below them. "How long will she kneel down there like that?"

"Until she falls over dead," Jaradan replied, the tone of his voice changing to show the serious nature of her question. "For one such as she, there is no going back. As you've said, she risks all by coming before you."

"Somebody must have mentioned you're back," he added, "I cannot think of a more noble gesture than to offer one's life."

"Sounds more foolhardy to me," Charley sighed, standing up as she continued to watch the girl, "Then again, I'm not one of those things you called her either."

"Portal Daemon," he replied quietly, "She knows the location of all the known portals, and perhaps a few of the unknown ones as well. She is not limited to those whose memories must be seen, or look at one of Anna's maps. Its unlikely one of her kind will be seen in the years that follow, they are very reclusive, greatly feared and respected. One of the tales told says that death itself touches the ground with one knee and bows at the passing of one such as she, such is her beauty and power."

"They're not great conversationalists."

"Portal Daemon … Death incarnate, I get the picture," Charley replied, glancing up at the threatening sky as more drops began to arrive around them before looking back down. "For how long?"

"Her quest? It lasts one earth year and a day in length, before she would be returned to her elders, her service complete," he replied, "It can continue for a lifetime if agreed on… depends," giving her a look. "She responds to threats to our side of reality, not just evil. Daemons stand guard."

"Whose lifetime, her's or mine?" Charley asked, raising an

eyebrow as she gave him a quick glance.

"Does it matter? The result is the same."

"True enough, stupid question," Charley let out with a long sigh, suddenly thinking on something, "How is she with those shape shifters we ran into?"

"Put it this way," Jaradan said, "If she had arrived earlier, you'd still be waiting to learn more of yourself."

"I think I'm learning something new just standing here looking at her," Charley said, "It seems the more I learn, the sooner the next lesson shows up," giving the waiting daemon a final glance before shifting her position.

"Of course, I might be mistaken," the gargoyle quietly mused to himself as he positioned himself to watch the encounter, "That just might be one of the old ones. They sort of look alike to me, maybe it was gold threads for the Noble houses, or was it blue robes and gold thread."

"I don't need anyone to work for me," she let out, dropping down onto her own knees to be at her level before the bowing figure, noting the subtle reaction to her words that seemed to ripple over the cloaked form.

"However," she continued with, "I can use someone who wishes to work with me at my side, a true member of a team. If this is acceptable to you, I return your sword," lifting the heavy blade from her by it's hilt as she stood up.

"If you wish to be tested by danger, I've been told you've come to the right place, just stand near me and it'll be wandering by sooner or later," holding it out before her. "We could have used you just the other day."

"I am in your service, Princess," she slowly let out, her low voice nearly taken away by the rising winds, a light tremble of relief showing as she slowly stood up, pulling her hood back from around her head before reaching out to take her sword back from Charley.

"Oh boy," Charley slowly let out, taking in the sight of her pale face, the heavy mass of white hair that began to show as the winds grabbed at it, her large coal black eyes that were fixed on Charley as she bowed before her once more, with her sword held tightly in one hand. "I've never seen a more beautiful Daemon," she added, taking a step backwards at the sight of her.

"Do you like blueberry pie?"

"What you looking at, the storm that's coming?" Georgie asked, noting Gretta interest in something outside. "It'll wash off the windows, save me the trouble."

"Portal Daemon, I think," Gretta let out quietly, giving him a glance before returning her attention to the sight outside on the walk. "In all my days, I've never seen one before."

"They're just stories to scare children with," he replied, giving a wave with one hand at what she had said, "All shrouded up creepy looking hags, as I heard it."

"Oh? I was told they are so beautiful that like the Sirens, they can attract anything to them, even death. Nothing alive can pass them if they set their mind to it. That's why they're covered up like that," she replied, her attention on the cloaked figure.

"You know how it is with creatures like that, the stories are so old that no one really knows the truth about them."

"The tale I heard says they're all shriveled up hump backs, and naked under them blue robes they wear. That's the real reason they wear them as they do. Keeps folks like me from fainting out on the streets," Georgie let out. "Isn't it lunch time around here?"

"It's a black robe, and I think we're going to need that extra pie, it's still baking in the oven," Gretta sighed, shaking her head at him as she led the way towards the kitchen, "They're headed this way."

"We're going to need to find us a proper baker."

"Told you they were all creepy looking, didn't I," Georgie whispered, as Gretta passed him to get another plate, glancing back at the hooded figure sitting at the far end of the table. "Don't ever tell me what they really look like, I don't want to think on it," he added, "The very thought scares me."

"She's got something to show you under her robe," Charley whispered, leaning over to join the conversation, "You won't believe your eyes when you see her, Georgie. Ask her to show you."

"I don't want to see her," he replied, keeping his voice low so he wouldn't be overheard, "The sight would just burn into my eyes, it'd haunt me… maybe make my heart stop."

"That's true," Charley said, slowly nodding her head at his remark, "It damn near stopped mine," giving Gretta a quick grin as she sat back up. "No sense in risking it."

"What's on your plate for this week," Gretta asked, carefully setting a plate down in front of the newest guest, giving Charley a glance as she began to serve large slices of the warm pie.

"I promised Sandi we'd go back to Washington, see the sites," Charley said, her eyes on the Daemon, letting out a wide smile as the girl took a tentative taste before taking the rest of it into her mouth. "I think she likes it."

"I can't keep up with demand on blueberry around here," Gretta let out, shaking her head as the hooded girl reached out and brought her plate closer to herself, "How about we try apple next. Warm, with ice cream and covered with extra cinnamon."

"Something tells me that idea isn't going to fly," Charley

let out slowly as everyone looked upwards at the sound of a low grumbling noise from somewhere above them. "Let's order them instead. I know these guys in Washington, they'll know where to go for them."

"Oh, it's you again," Simmons let out, rubbing at one eye as he answered the knocking at his door, "What brings the little red haired girl to my door... at freaking midnight."

"On tour, there aren't any crowds this time of day," Charley quipped, giving him a smile. "Got your info from Agent Rodgers, he knew where you lived."

"He was happier to see us though," Sandi said, crossing her arms as she gave him a look.

"Oh, not you, too," Simmons sighed, shaking his head. "To what do I owe the pleasure?"

"Who the hell is that?" he suddenly asked, finally noticing the dark figure standing silently to one side, "Yet another team girl?"

"Yep, and she wants to know where that place is you picked up those blueberry pies from," Charley replied, "You know, that last time we were here?"

"She's worked up an appetite, some mugger jumped out from this alleyway on 17th Street, on the way over here. Thought she had a purse to snatch I guess."

"Some desperate soul," Sandi added, nodding her head. "I left my kitty at home, we were left unprotected. A prime target."

"You're out trolling the streets of Washington... with the likes of her, a living avenger," Simmons said, looking at the cloaked figure with a faint expression of anxiety for a moment before giving Charley his attention, "and you've come to me asking for pie. What kind of operation are you running?"

"Girl's night out," Charley replied, showing him a sweet smile. "Now, about those pies," reaching out to give him a pat on one shoulder, "We need to be on our way."

"Why me," he sighed, tightening the belt on his robe before hesitantly taking a step back to let them in, his attention fixed on the dark form as she silently passed him. "Keep that one on a leash. What did I do to deserve this?"

"Karma," Sandi said, looking around his apartment as they followed him into the living room. "Nice. Small, but not that bad."

"Thanks, I'll wait for the award to arrive in the mail," he said, walking over to one of the two tables that flanked the sofa. "I've got the card around here somewhere, hard to remember that far back," suddenly letting out a deep snarl of rage as he caught the subtle movement of the slinking leopard as it crept up behind him, his head continuing to move as it fell down on the carpet with a thump as he tried to make a desperate leap towards Charley with claws extended, the rest of his body quickly following it.

"Impressive," Sandi let out, admiring the gleaming sword as it was returned to the folds of her cloak.

"Told you there were two of them," Charley sighed, taking a step back as she looked down at the spreading ooze coming from the creature on the floor as May and Rodgers entered with several other men quickly following them, their weapons out and ready. "Nice, a Master, and two slaves. We caught this one unawares, he wasn't ready for us. Perfect timing."

"The real Simmons is upstairs, he's lying up there in the bedroom," May added, noting Rodger's expression as the daemon quietly turned to look his way, her face hidden in shadows. "He's still alive, but his breathing sounds ragged. He'll need some medical care."

"That one's scary," Rodgers let out, giving the cloaked girl a glance, before looking back down at the creature on the floor as put his weapon away to bring out his cell phone, "Simmons is going to need his carpet replaced," waving a hand at the now rising stench. "Carlson's going to just love this."

"He pays the piper on this one," Charley said, giving the carpet another quick glance before looking over at him. "I had to hire a specialist. We might have had our hands full if this thing hadn't gotten petrified at the sight of our newest team member."

"Go ahead and take out what it costs for Simmons to get new carpet in here, I'll cover that, but he's on his own with any doctor bills. I don't get paid all that much you know."

"Hey, did you guys remember to bring my pies with you?"

"Did you get an image on where he came from?" Anna asked, setting a folder down as they gathered around her desk.

"Sure did," Charley replied, smiling at her. "I can't say that thing was working for the same one that Harold was so scared of, but it's one more we can rid ourselves of, now that we have a starting point."

"We can't wait long, once the fate of that last changer becomes known it'll be expecting us," Summer said, setting a pie box down on Anna's desk, smiling at Granddon's interested glance as he sniffed the air.

"Might be one of those knock down drag out fights," Summer offered up, "It could be get real nasty this time."

"All the more reason to take him out soon," Charley said, looking from her over to Anna. "I'm taking two teams in with me."

"The grapevine is saying you've got another member," Anna let out, sitting down at her desk and picking up her pen to tap the side of her face as she leaned back to give Charley a thoughtful look. "I don't want to know where you found her. One of the tales I heard says they know the portal to hell itself."

"It's a mystery," Charley replied, showing her a smile, "Like the rest of everything else in my life, including my bank account. I realized after awhile that I don't get any statements from the bank, so I went down there on my lunch break."

"Yes?" Anna said, raising an eyebrow.

"It seems the balance in there doesn't change... ever. It's still the amount you said was setup for me when I took the job."

"Ah, maybe your account is broken. Would you like me to fix it for you?" Anna asked, still sitting back in her chair to await her reply.

"Oh, no no no," I was just using that as an example of some of the mystery that goes on around here," Charley quickly said, waving a hand in the air at the question. "It seems to be running just fine. If it isn't broken, don't fix it."

"Good idea," Anna muttered, hiding her smile as she leaned forward, picking the folder back up to hold it out, "He's one of the bad boys, so there's no reason to ask him any questions, or play with feathers on this one."

"I see this one as be quick, or be dead," she added, "You might want to pack a lunch, it's unlikely he's alone. Your team up for that?"

"Isn't this what you pay me for?" Charley let out, taking the folder from her, "We'll get going soon. I have the image from old stinky to go by."

"Where's the big boy, he's usually standing behind you at times like this," Anna suddenly asked, glancing around the office for the gargoyle.

"Making battle plans, just in case this one is bulletproof, too." Charles said, glancing over the report, "As you've said, we need to do our homework on this one."

"Well, I've got five other teams on standby, all volunteers," Anna said, "Don't get cute and take on too much."

"So I see," Charley let out in a low voice as she scanned over the contents of the folder, "They all wanted to kick some evil butt?"

"No, it seems they all wanted to work with you when they heard you had another mission," Anna replied, shaking her head, "Don't ask me why. My mental capacity is limited, I must have missed breakfast."

"Tell them to gear up, we're going in at midnight," Charley said, giving her watch a glance, "I'll give you a call if we need them."

"Who volunteered first?"

"Spider team," Anna said, showing a slight shudder, "They're not local, so don't go expecting the small variety."

"Oh?" Charley let out, holding her hands about a foot apart before widening to two feet as she gave Anna a questioning look.

"They can bring down a running Yak with ease. The ring bearer claims they hunt something like hippos on their off time… for practice. They hunt in pairs," Anna said, raising an eyebrow as she leaned back in her chair. "Big enough?"

"Poisonous too?" Charley asked, her eyes widening at the mental picture.

"Oh, you betcha," Anna said, beginning to show a smile, "and they sort of look like a hairy tarantula. Want to hear about the team that reminds me of a walking octopus? They've just come in from one of the outer rings. Great swimmers."

"I think I'll save that one for later, we have to be off to a late lunch," Charley quickly replied shaking her head. "We're off to the Steak Barn, its sunset."

"Does De'mone know how to talk?" Jacob whispered over, keeping his eyes on the cloaked figure. "She's awfully quiet over there, cute too. I got a glimpse of her face when we all came in."

"She's not much of a talker. She's a foreigner, that's why she keeps herself all covered up like that," Charley whispered back, following his gaze over to the Daemon. "She's just trying out all the new foods here while she's here. I'm not sure if they have baked potato and steak where she's from. You're right though, she's a real cutie."

"Is she some kind of hump back or something? I thought I saw her robe move," he asked, trying not to be obvious as he gave her another glance, "You think she might want come over and watch a movie with us?"

"How's the new bike working out for you? Like it?" Charley asked, returning her attention back to her own plate as she changed the topic.

"That thing is just great," Jacob let out excitedly, taking a quick drink to keep from choking on his own meal. "Nobody else around has one, zooms right along. It's got my old bike beat all hollow."

"I guess my mom tossed it out, the junk man must have hauled it off 'cause I couldn't find it when I went looking. I guess it reminded her of how I got hurt on it."

"Yeah, no sense cluttering that garage you guys have either," Charley remarked, showing a smile, "Before long you'll be needing the room for a motorcycle."

"Like that's going to happen," Jacob let out, shaking his head at the thought. "I don't think so."

"Stranger things have been known to happen," Charley said, giving him a smile. "One never knows."

"School starts next Monday, we riding together in your new car like you said," he asked looking back over to her.

"Sure are, no more school bus for us. You can meet me at my place, or I'll pick you up," she replied. "Walsh is going to swallow his tongue when he sees us getting out."

"Yeah, that jerk can eat his heart out," Jacob sighed. "I can't wait to see their faces."

"No movies tonight, sorry to say," Charley said, showing him a sad expression. "It's a girl's night out this evening, it's all been planned out. Maybe we can plan something for Saturday, we'll have us a cookout or something."

"Oh…" Jacob quietly let out, trying not to stare at the sight as the Daemon reached up, tugging on her hood to reveal her face to him, showing him a smile as the dessert was being brought to their table. "She's a model, too," he finally gave out, the beauty of her face almost causing him to stammer. "Can I have a photo of her?"

"Oh, you'll have to ask her on that," Charley quietly replied, smiling at his reaction. "I heard that she's naked under there. You'd have to hide it."

"Right next to the winter edition that's coming out later," she added. "That's the one with me on the white bear skin rug. You're going to have a rare collection."

Chapter Eleven

"Oh, Teddy," Charley let out bending down to pick up the stuffed bear lying in the middle of the hallway, "What are you doing here? I thought I left you standing guard in my bedroom," brushing at the fur with one hand. "You'll get dirty in here."

"I'll just have to keep an eye on you after this," she muttered, making sure he was clean, before tucking the bear under one arm as she walked further down the dimly light corridor, "We'd be lost in here in here if I didn't have the glow from this pendant I'm wearing to help out."

"I'm tired, Teddy," finally giving out a long sigh, leaning against one wall as she peered down another dim hall that she found before her after stumbling for the second time. "Too many choices, and I can't seem to remember what I'm looking for anymore. I don't like the way this place smells, it makes me dizzy."

"Oh, wait," turning her head to listen to a faint sound ahead of her, "That sounds like running water."

"Oh, it's a pool," she slowly let out, taking in small waterfall that emptied into a deep body of water as the end of the hall opened up before her and she found herself outside. Mesmerized by the sight, she walked forward, ending up on a grassy area at the water's edge.

"You get to rest up, too," she muttered, dropping the stuffed bear down beside her feet as she kept her eyes on the faint surface images on the water that seemed to appear, only to vanish once more as the swirls from the nearby falls took them away.

"Faces, strange pancake faces," Charley finally said quietly, a frown coming to her face as she gave another image her attention, noting the dark eyes that seemed to be watching her as it passed her by, it's mouth making motions as if speaking her with no sounds that she could hear.

Kneeling down, she leaning over and reached out to poke one of the faces with a finger as it came her way, the form on the water moving around her finger, its eyes following her as it too, passed by. "It's as if I know them from somewhere, Teddy."

"I should go swimming," she said, looking across the water for a moment before giving the bear a glance. "I've gone swimming before... I'm just too tired to remember where. It'll wake me up, it'll be refreshing," standing back up to look around her.

"What's that, Teddy? I'd disturb the faces?" she let out quietly, her attention still on the water.

"I don't care, they can all go somewhere else to swim now," she finally said, dropping to her knees. "Here, keep an eye on this for me, placing pendent around the bear's neck.

"Whoa, hold on there," a voice said, coming to her from the darkness she struggled to emerge from, "You're not doing well."

Shaking off the hands that had tried to hold her still, Charley managed to open her eyes, trying to take in her blurred surroundings as she looked around her. "What the hell happened," doing her best to focus on the boy she discovered sitting near her.

"You were screaming something, you lost your necklace when you began to thrash about," he said, moving further away as she sat up, "I didn't know what to do."

"Oh, my head," Charley let out, holding her hands to her forehead in an attempt to ease the dizziness, "I don't feel so good."

"There's a sink, over there," the boy hastily said, pointing across to the other side of the small room, eyeing her as Charley promptly made a dive for it, the contents of her stomach quickly erupting as she turned the water on.

"Here, your necklace," he said holding it out as she reclaimed a seat on the cot she had woken up on.

"I don't want it," pushing at it. "I think I'm going to faint," coming out as he held a hand against her back, rubbing slowing at her shoulders.

His eyes impassive, he let her slump over, the pendent falling from her hands to land back down on the floor. "Let's try something else, sweet girl," his tone of voice shifting while reaching down once more to pick the necklace up, giving her his attention for a moment as he produced another from his pocket, exchanging it with the one he was holding.

"You shouldn't lose this one, so lets just tuck it away somewhere, shall we," he suddenly came out with, his eyes changing as he reached down to tug at the zipper of her tunic, bringing it halfway down to display the swell of her breasts in the gap of the opening.

Taking the new pendent, he carefully removed the chain from around the dull crystal, giving out a light smile as he then tried to slide it in, only to discover, to his disgust, the body armor prevented his hand from finding a bare breast. Pulling at the zipper to bring it halfway back up, he used that to hold the crystal in place. "There," he sighed, the memory of her lingering in his mind, his thoughts reaching out to consider the rest of her form as he gave her another look, "Let's see if it stays in place there."

"I'll have to check it later of course, we don't want you to loose it," reaching out to run a hand down over her hair, lingering once more at the gentle swell of her cleavage, "When we have more time, we'll just have to make you more comfortable, but someone's coming," giving a look towards the door.

Standing up, he gave her a final glance before turning to open the door. Behind him, Charley gave out a low moan as the crystal slowly reacted to the touch of her skin, producing a dim glow as it began to send out subtle ripples of energy across her.

Smiling at the first beads of sweat that appeared, he gave a out a quiet laugh, his eyes darkening again briefly, before showing a frown as he closed the door behind him, making his way quickly down the hallway.

Letting out a deep sigh, Charley slowly allowed a feeling to bring her from the fog that had filled her mind, reveling beneath the gentle soft touch against her, the touch repeating until it had reached her zipper.

With a sudden gasp, she was brought out from the depths of her mind with a deep moan that racked her body, bringing her up right with a start, the crystal that had been lying against her falling aside as the tentacle struck at it again, sending it flying from her body just as the door bulged inwards from a mighty blow. Wrenched outwards, the pieces flew through the air as Jaradan let out a loud roar of discovery.

"About time," Charley managed to get out with a dry voice,

struggling to stand up, "Thanks Ralphie," giving the tentacled blob a quick glance before she wavered, quickly sitting back down to recover.

"What happened?" she asked tugging on her zipper before giving up, simply to weak to close it any better than it was.

"You mean while you were lounging around in here," the gargoyle replied, giving the room a quick check, "Lots, Princess. Portal jumps, monsters... you name it. Our new team member was the one who finally figured it out," stepping over to run some water into a cupped hand as he looked over at her, "He employed a Dream Weaver."

"Here," splashing the cold water on her face, "Snap out it, time to go to work."

"Wow," Charley let out, reacting to the water with a wide-eyed expression, "Thanks, I think," regaining her feet as she wiped at her eyes. "Where are the teams?"

"He was using some sort of tunnels, not the kind in the dirt," he added as he led them down the corridor outside of her room, "Time and matter, something to do with tears in the fabric of space as I understand it. Real sneaky bastard."

"What's in that room there?" Charlie asked, another doorway catching her attention as they passed, the opening also wrenched aside, as if by some great beast.

"You don't want to know," Jaradan rumbled, glancing around as they made their way into another room. "A fate worse than death. Evil things."

"Let's track this guy down," noting the look in the gargoyles eyes, "There's too much evil in the world these days."

"It's an illusion," Jaradan quickly said, seeing her suddenly stop at the edge of the crevasse that suddenly opened before them, "He has some abilities, and he's had some practice using it," he added, grabbing one of her hands as he stepped out, his feet still firmly on the stone tiled floor, "We're learning what they are, and how to deal with them as we go. Slowed us down at first, sorry."

"That's alright, I wasn't doing anything in particular, just lounging around," Charlie replied, glancing around the room they found themselves in. "Where did he go?"

"There," Sandi called out, panting for breath as she appeared at the opening of another doorway across from them, looking around the large den like room before pointing towards a large mural that covered the far wall, "That must be the one."

"Oh, man, don't ever do that again," suddenly letting out with a loud groan as she was brushed aside from behind, the huge spider quickly moving silently past her as it made it way into the room ahead of her.

"My fault, Ghost," a boy's voice replied, his head appearing around from the other side of the door frame, "we're on the scent," as a second spider crept past Sandi to join the first one, "He went in there, your tiger's right on his tail."

"He isn't a tiger," Sandi managed to get out, holding a hand on her chest in an attempt to get her breathing slowed back down, "he's a leopard. I can see what he does, and it's been nothing but spiders."

"Oh, excuse me, they just look like spiders," the boy retorted, smiling as he passed her, pausing briefly to give her a pat on one arm, "Come on you cute Ghost thing, we're catching up."

"Was that a younger version of Hercules that I just saw?" Charlie asked, staring in wonder at the boy that had just entered the room across from them.

"So it would seem," Jaradan let out, his eyes narrowing as he gave the wall-sized mural his attention, "This one takes us back."

"I want a pay raise after this one," Sandi muttered, following along behind the spiders as the first one paused before the wall, then stepped in it, a shimmer rippling across the image as it vanished from sight, quickly followed by the other one and then the young man who commanded them.

"Spider Team," Jaradan said quietly, noting Charlie's expression, "he's got Sandi's heart all aflutter."

"Tell me something I don't know," she let out, giving him a smack with one hand, "Come on, he's getting away," leading them towards the mural.

"You said back," Charlie said, following behind the gargoyle as he paused outside the mural to hold a hand for her, "Back where?"

"To where we found him the first time, back where May and Summer are on watch. Back where he put the whammy on you with that crystal trick of his," Jaradan replied, holding her hand as they too vanished in to the portal.

"Actually, it wasn't his crystal," Summer said, correcting him as they appeared, "It belongs to his boss, the one Harold was so scared of."

"We figured it out," May added, handing Charley's weapon back over to her, "It was planted with us, allowing him to use some of your own energy against yourself. He isn't strong enough on his own."

"Ah, clever," Charley mused, checking to see if her gun was loaded before replacing it on her belt, "Man, is it nice to see you guys again. Who's this other one we're chasing?"

"Another of his minions, from what I can tell," May replied, eyeing Charley's stuck zipper with a raised eyebrow, "Bad news in his own right. He got left behind with the Dream Weaver, trying to get you out of the picture."

"Where's our Daemon girl," looking around the room they found themselves in.

"Oh, that one got upset, and no one was very interested in stopping her," May replied, her eyes widening at the memory, "She went after the boss. We split up, she left his underlings and your search to us, took *Ryuu* with her. She's ambitious, wants to guard the portal to hell the way she's going."

"Tracking you down took awhile, he kept moving, always one step ahead of us at each turn," Jaradan remarked, giving the room his attention, "The Dream Weaver got herself flamed, you missed it."

"We used your locator," Sandi explained, entering in to the room from another open arched doorway, "He's hiding around here somewhere, look sharp people. I don't know, but he might have changed his form again. He's hiding somewhere where it's dark."

"Stand back," Jaradan suddenly called out, reaching out to pull Charley to one side as the thick wooden pillars adorning the corners of the doorway gave out a horrendous groan, snapping in half under the weight of the two battling spiders as they came crashing down from the ceiling, the crushed plaster sending a white dust cloud around the room as an intense battle ensured on the cracked and broken tiles of the floor.

"Can't see a damn thing," Charley called out, holding her weapon at the ready, her attention on the mass of fighting confusion that ensued before her.

"Give it a minute," Sandi replied, from the other side of the battle, watching in awe as her leopard came crashing through the wall panel beside her, adding to the dust as he joined the foray, "We're winning."

"We got his ass," Bronson, the younger man who commanded the spiders called out, peering down from the hole in the ceiling above them, "He's toast."

"Jaradan, how about we sever the head from the body,

one never knows," Charley finally came out with, staring at the oddly shaped form on the floor for a few minutes before giving the gargoyle her attention, "Maybe the poison wears off after we turn our backs on it. I don't want this thing sitting back up after we've left."

"Not a bad idea," Sandi said, agreeing with her as she stood with hands on hips, a look of disgust on her face, "One down, one still out there."

"Well, what are we waiting for," Charley remarked, a smile coming to her face as she put her weapon away, "Let's go get him, maybe he's got friends. No reason to let them daemons have all the fun around here."

"You might want to use these," Sandi said, holding out a set of goggles, "Night vision, in case we're working in the dark, I borrowed a couple from Granddon. It seems we're the only ones that need them."

"We're close," Charley remarked, sighting the oozing bodies they were forced to step over, as they made their way down the passageway.

"Decision time," Jaradan muttered, noting the junction ahead of them, "Do we go right, or left?"

"There's something waiting for us down this one," Brandon came out with, coming up to join them as they paused, "My team can sense them."

"Evil lurks down that way," May added, nodding to Charley, "He's right, something is waiting for us."

"We split up then," Charley decided, giving Sandi a nod, "Your team takes point," nodding to the left passage. "Take Spider team, for some reason I feel better when I know they're not crawling up behind me in a dark tunnel," giving Bronson a quick grin.

"The rest of us go to the right, use the locators if we get cut off from each other in this maze," looking around at them, "We'll make our own tunnel, if we have too."

"We're not interested in taking any prisoners."

"Did you guys just see something move?" Charley asked quietly, trying to peer into the dimly lit chamber that opened up before them.

"Well, we know *Ryuu* didn't come in this way, so there must be another entrance to where this guy is holed up," Jaradan remarked, noting the lack of scorch marks on the walls.

"It must cold blooded, I'm not sensing much of it," Summer noted, coming up beside Charley to use her better night vision, "and it's big," craning her head upwards as she tried to take in the entire creature facing them.

"Well," May remarked, joining her sister at the opening, "That's not something you see everyday."

"It looks like a giant crab," Jaradan came out with, trying to press Charley aside so he could get his bulk through to the opening, "I'll take care of it."

"Since when do you eat crab meat," Charley came out with, reaching out to grab one wrist as the gargoyle tried to force himself past her, "I know what happens when you stick them in the pot, you know."

"That's quite a grip you've developed," he remarked, trying to free himself from her grasp without success, "Let me go, there's work to be done."

"This isn't some illusion," May noted, sliding back to let Charley move closer, "Those claws could do some real damage."

"Watch this," Charley let out, lowering herself down on her knees ahead of Jaradan, while lifting up a hand, palm up.

With widening eyes, May and Summer watched in surprise as a small sparkle of light appeared in the middle of her open hand, the low brief flicker growing stronger as Charley gained confidence in her abilities, "I found my mother's diary in her room," she let out in a low voice, her attention on the now dancing flame she held, "I've only skimmed over some of the entries, but I remember this. Here goes nothing."

Raising her palm higher, she took in a deep breath, letting it out with a loud whoosh that sent the red flames changing into an intense light blue as it suddenly expanded, filling the entire room before them in hot, brilliant waves of energy.

"Nice trick," the gargoyle admitted, giving Charley a glance as he pushed the remaining sections of the carcass aside so that they could gain access to the arched doorway on the other side of the chamber.

"I'm just full of surprises," Charley quipped, peering ahead of them, "I think we're getting closer, there's a trail of evil in the air ahead of us. I think that thing was placed there to slow us down."

"Wow, we all just went through a hidden portal," May announced, giving herself a slight shudder from the feeling that had swept over her, "We've changed locations. I hope the others can follow us."

"What is this place?" May asked, looking around them at the thick wooden doors, "There's a strange light in the air here."

"Looks like storerooms, maybe we ended up in someone's basement," Summer remarked, giving the closest one a quick check, "It smells sweet, like old spices."

"Weird, I can't wait to catch up with this guy," Charley muttered, leading them on, further down towards a set of stone steps that led upwards from the passageway she discovered at the far end, "Shame we don't have a picture to go by."

"What a strange place," Charley remarked, as they all entered the first chamber on the next floor, looking around them at the ancient markings on the walls, "I'm getting a funny feeling, it's beginning to have a unexpected familiar touch to it."

"They're kind of hard to make out," Jaradan muttered, wiping at one of the dust covered markings, "It's old, been here almost forever from the looks of this," noting the large shrouded mirror sitting against one of the far walls, set into a small almost alcove like space, "Must be one of the old portals," glancing around at the other walls, a thought coming to him as he glanced from one set of markings to another, "Oh," he quietly muttered to himself, "Boy, how soon we forget," giving the room another look, giving Charley a thoughtful furtive glance as he brushed his hands together.

"Wow, take a look at these," May let out as she walked in to the adjoining room that lead off from the first chamber, looking around in awe at the huge embroidered tapestries that covered the walls, "That looks like threads of gold," pointing at the one hanging to her right. "I think these all tell stories," peering closer at the faint images, "Hard to make out, this place could use a good cleaning. Everything's covered in this dust."

"This isn't his place, he still trying to slow us down. He must be getting desperate," Jaradan slowing came out with, catching up behind the rest of the group as they filed through the corridor to follow May.

"Man, this place is incredible," Charley said, glancing over at the tall, ancient looking silver candle holders that sat at the entrance of each of arched doorways, as they walked along,

"I don't think anybody lives here, everything is covered with dust."

"Whoever it was, they had good tastes," Summer remarked, glancing into another dim room as they passed by, "Antiques everywhere you look, the statues and carvings on the interior walls are high quality, looks like a labor of love to me."

"This all feels like someone moved out, leaving everything as it was," Charley said, still taking in the other wall hangings as they walked down the length of the passageway, "It has this odd kind of feel to it," pausing for a moment to glance back at the gargoyle, "like I've seen these tapestries somewhere before, like in a dream."

"Looks like he used that old portal back there to escape whatever was on his tail," Jaradan remarked, coming up beside Charley, "See," pointing out the footprints scuffed in the dust on the tiled floor, "Somebody was in a big hurry, running from the looks of it."

"As if something was right on his tail," Charley let out, following the trail with her eyes as it went down the hall, "I only see one set of foot prints."

"Movement," May called out, holding up one hand in warning as she looked ahead towards another opening.

"It's *Ryuu*," she reported, turning to give Charley a quick glance, "She has everyone else with her. They're coming out from the corridor on the other side."

"Did you check out that statue standing back there?" Sandi came out with, as she came up to them, gestured back the way they had come, "A lady, must be ten feet tall and made of solid gold," she gushed. "You've got to see her, all she's wearing is a wide sweeping cloak around her shoulders, and the detail is absolutely incredible… reminds me of someone."

"How did you guys get here?" Charley asked, holding up a

hand, turning to Ryuu for an explanation.

"I was sent back to lead them, we just missed you," the dragon replied, motioning towards the end of the hall with her head, "We need to go that way, she's got him cornered in the Great Hall."

"We'll get the tour later," Charley quickly replied, giving Sandi a fast glance as she gave out a wave with one hand, leading them in the direction the dragon had indicated.

"This way, I can feel him now," Charley let out in a loud voice, taking the wide steps upwards two at a time as she picked up the pace. "We're close, guys."

"We're too late," Jaradan came out with, as they all came to an abrupt stop at the edge the dais that the High Throne sat upon, "He's over there."

"She's got him cornered, alright," Sandi remarked, making sure her leopard was remaining at her side, unwilling to commit him to the battle unfolding before them.

"He's toast," Bronson remarked, coming up behind Charley, his spiders in trail, "You girls might want to lose those goggles now, it's not dark in here."

Her attention on the two before them, Charley slowly reached up to give her goggles a tug, letting them fall down around her neck, her eyes widening as the full, brilliant colors of the room surprised her. "Oh, wow. I know where we are."

"It's red," she quietly exclaimed, raising her hands to peer at the dust that still covered her fingers, "It just looked gray with the goggles, it was red the whole time," looking back to the figures ahead of them, "I'm back."

"There's something I should have mentioned about that daemon," Jaradan came out with, watching with satisfaction as the man facing her tried to escape, moving upwards several steps, his back against the ancient marble slabs so he could still see his pursuer.

"Interesting," Charley replied, her attention now on the daemon with sword in hand, ripples of energy running down the blade as she spread open her wings, her entire form taking on a pastel violet hue as the very air around her shimmered with a palpable energy.

Hair loose and flowing around her as if it was alive, the waves moved over her bare form in a constant, almost fluid like sensuous motion, it's length swirling past her knees as she stood before him with smoldering dark eyes.

"You can save me," the man suddenly called out, looking towards Charley with a look of desperation, his hands clutching at the smooth surface of the marble as he slowly moved away from the sight that stood before, his legs beginning to tremble from fear.

"I can tell you everything," he hastily shouted, his eyes moving from side to side as he sought a means of escape, "Kill me and you'll never learn who you are."

"I was there, I know," he added, seeing Charley expression change.

"You didn't tell me everything," Charley remarked, giving the gargoyle beside her a quick glance, before returning her attention to the two before saying anything else. "Something tells me that's not a Portal Daemon."

"You're right," Jaradan admitted, lifting his hands up to slow any further remarks concerning his error, "She's an Avenging Angel, my bad."

"That's the one who gave me that look, the day I went in to apply for the job," Charley noted, now remembering where she had seen him before, "He was after me before I was even on the clock."

"He preys on the innocent," Jaradan remarked, nodding his

head, "I wasn't in a position to do anything."

"Oh, don't go blaming yourself, I wasn't either," Charley mused, her attention on the cowering figure on the steps above them, "Does one of the most evil creatures I've ever encountered still speak the truth?"

"Whatever he would say would only be twisted to prevent his own demise," Sandi remarked, her own attention on the sight of the Angel, "That's his nature."

"Yes, I suppose you're right," Charley replied, "What knowledge I might gain in his fear would only be tainted by his own selfish needs. I don't need a list of his victims either, I have other things to read in my spare time. School starts on Monday."

"Finish your task," Charley suddenly called out to the Angel, still poised with sword in hand, "There are others in the universe that call out in need, evil never sleeps."

"I find that the adventure that comes with seeking them out is exciting," turning to look at the gargoyle, "It's actually not a bad job to have. I'm not saying we won't be getting our hands dirty from time to time," brushing her own hands together in an attempt to rid herself of the dust, "But I like the way I feel once the job's finished."

"Are you going to tell me the rest of the story," giving Jaradan her attention as they headed back towards the main entrance to the temple, "Everything he was holding onto as a bargaining chip. I didn't buy that little desperation act, he thought it would save his own hide. That's how evil acts."

"Ahh," taking a step back as he considered her request as the other members of the teams gathered around them to hear his response, "Would you like to see your statue?"

"I'm worn out," Charley let out, letting herself drop down

on the office sofa, facing Anna, "Sorry about the dust, it's been one of those days."

"You seem to have gotten the best of the situation," Anna replied, sliding a folder over to one side of her desk as she turned her attention to Charley.

"Well, learned a lot," Charley replied, showing a faint smile, "I should go soak in a hot tub somewhere."

"Well, can't stay. It's time I got these tired bones back home," she added, letting out a light yawn, before regaining her feet, "the hour grows late."

"Great, I'll have everything ready for tomorrow," Anna remarked, showing a smile, "Training's over, Princess."

"Yeah, I guess it is," she replied, her smile widening at the remark, "I should let you know, I've been reading the diary left up my room, the one with no key."

"Yes?" Anna replied, lifting an eyebrow as she waited for more.

"There is no will," Charley finally gave out, glancing around the office for a moment before looking back over to Anna, "I'm taking tomorrow off, I've got school in the morning. I can give you a note from the boss, if you need one."

"Wow, this place is cool looking," the dark haired girl let out, slowly stepping out from the elevator to peer around the office before noticing Charley sitting quietly at the desk.

"Hey there, I'm Amanda. I'm here about the job. Man, did you see that abominable snowman figure down they got down there in the lobby?" she asked while walking over, "Incredible detail, must be seven feet tall and covered with this deep white soft fur. It's eyes sort of stare at you as you walk by."

"Sounds like a Yeti, alright," Charley said quietly, sitting back in her chair, holding her pen to her lips as she gave the girl her attention. "They tend to move those things around down there, so I haven't had a chance to check it out yet. You'd never believe what was down there before," opening up the folder lying on the desktop.

"I'm Charley, I'm here filling in for a few days. The regular girl is off on her honeymoon. Married some guy from the FBI, if you can believe that. I'm always the last one to get told these things around here."

"Like Yeti's do you?" Charley asked, giving the girl an appraising look, leaning forward at the nod she gave.

"Did you bring the sign?"

The End

Would you like to see your manuscript become a book?

If you are interested in becoming a PublishAmerica author, please submit your manuscript for possible publication to us at:

acquisitions@publishamerica.com

You may also mail in your manuscript to:

**PublishAmerica
PO Box 151
Frederick, MD 21705**

www.publishamerica.com

PUBLISHAMERICA

CPSIA information can be obtained at www.ICGtesting.com
Printed in the USA
269703BV00001B/42/P

9 781462 633173